HIDDEN SECRETS

An Agnes Barton Senior Sleuths Mystery

MADISON JOHNS

Copyright © 2018 Madison Johns
Hidden Secrets Madison Johns
All rights reserved.

Created with Vellum

This is a work of fiction. Names, characters, businesses, places, events and incidents are either the products of the author's imagination or used in a fictitious manner. Any resemblance to actual persons, living or dead, or actual events is purely coincidental.

No part of this publication may be reproduced, distributed or transmitted in any form or by any means, including photocopying, recording or other electronic or mechanical methods, without the prior written permission of the publisher, except in the case of brief quotations embodied in critical reviews and certain other noncommercial uses permitted by copyright law.

SYNOPSIS

Life in Tawas has changed dramatically when Bernice "The Cat Lady's" ex-husband Wilber goes missing and is later found dead by resident detectives Agnes Barton and Eleanor Mason. Bernice is a suspect and the sleuths can't let their friend down as they search for the truth. Oh and about that truth -- who was Wilber really, and what secrets did he keep hidden throughout the years?

Wilber has been linked to a series of missing hitchhikers in the seventies. Has someone from the past come back for their revenge? Was Wilber really a serial killer? Will the girls be able to solve this case as a health crisis strikes down one of their friends?

This is one twisty tale.

CHAPTER 1

I stared down at the tiny kittens on my couch where Duchess had decided to give birth. I had resolved to throw my couch out, but my husband Andrew assured me it could be reupholstered. I had to admit the kittens were cute, and Duchess was a dutiful mother, but I couldn't possibly keep them all.

I'm Agnes Barton and I investigate crimes in Tawas, Mich., with my partner Eleanor Mason. We're senior sleuths, both over the age of seventy, but that has never stopped us from investigating. Far from it. We're retired and what else can retired ladies do to while away their day? I tried my hand at gardening once, but it's so much more enjoyable chasing down clues.

I brushed my salt and pepper hair and smiled, revealing a set of new dentures. My last pair was virtually useless they were so ground down. The wrinkles that I once considered marring my face I have now grown to accept. I jokingly blame Eleanor for most of them, but I met her only four years ago and most of my lines are much older.

"Agnes," Andrew greeted as he walked in the door with a golf club, a worrying frown on his face.

"Did you go golfing with the Hayes this morning?" I asked.

Andrew shook his head. "I planned to, but when I arrived at the club my favorite golf club was bent. I don't suppose you know anything about it?"

"Why would I?"

Andrew smiled, resembling the gray fox every woman over the age of thirty admired. My husband only has eyes for me and me him. I was so fortunate to call him mine even though we married only a few years ago. He was a former boss, one I admired very much. He was married at the time and I was a lonely widow, but nothing came of it back then. We reconnected in a big way when he arrived in Tawas for a brief visit a few years ago.

"I can't tell you the last time I even saw your clubs."

Andrew smiled and pulled out a pitcher of lemonade and poured a glass. "It will give me an excuse to shop for a new set. Bill Hayes has already volunteered to help me."

"That wouldn't surprise me." Bill and his wife Marjory are the biggest golfers I know. They practically live at the golf club during the season.

I picked up the phone when it rang and nodded with a smile. "I'll be right there, Eleanor." Once I ended the call I added, "You know Eleanor, she couldn't survive a day without me."

"I don't believe either of you could away from each other. I look forward to you coming home later and telling me about the lack of a crime here in Tawas."

"Do you think we go looking for crime? Because I most certainly do not. We just have a habit of finding it wherever we go."

"Whoever gets home first makes dinner," he joked as he rustled through the closet and replaced his bent golf club before jogging out the door.

Andrew didn't need a new set of golf clubs at all. But I suppose buying them might equate to a woman coloring her hair or buying new clothes. It makes me the tiniest bit giddy whenever I bring new purchases home.

I filled Duchess's food dish before I grabbed my handbag and hopped in my Mustang. I was trying to sell the car because I have such a hard time climbing out of it. Andrew promised to help me pick out a sedan more suited to my needs. Eleanor and I usually zoomed around in her old Cadillac if Andrew's SUV wasn't available. That Cadillac was like a tank and had gotten Eleanor and me out of some serious jams.

I admired Tawas Bay as I wound my way up U.S. 23. I had to pinch myself every time I thought about living here. I wasn't able to swing a lakeside house, but Eleanor inherited her cabin on the lake from a nephew who'd died some time ago.

Eleanor opened the door before I even had a chance to get out of my car.

"It's about time you got here," she called out with a smile.

"I hope you have coffee," I said as I climbed out of the car.

"You mean we can't go to Tim Hortons and get a cup?"

"I'm bored with doing that if you want to know. And my clothing is getting snugger."

"Maybe if we only had coffee and not the doughnuts we'd be okay." She laughed, her generous stomach bouncing in time. "I don't worry about my figure. I've always been a plus-sized woman. That's politically correct for fat."

"I know, but I've never seen you that way or would judge you for it." I glanced around. "Where is Mr. Wilson?" Mr. Wilson, Eleanor's husband, wouldn't allow anyone to use his first name.

"On the deck sleeping, most likely. It's time for my yearly blood draw."

"You're relatively healthy, Eleanor. My doctor has me go four times a year."

"Mine does too, but I always lose my lab slip or find it only to lose it again. My memory has been horrible."

"It can't be any worse than mine."

I continued through the opened patio door, and indeed Mr. Wilson was sawing logs in a lounge chair. He was wearing what he always wore, gray pants and a button-down shirt. They were the same kind of clothes he wore when he worked. Some habits are hard to break. Wilson's emaciated body and gray skin would make people think he's sick, but he's been knocking on death's door for years now. In truth, he managed quite well and only required the use of a rolling walker for assistance.

I yawned as I turned back to Eleanor. "So what do you feel like doing today?"

"I don't know. It's been so boring of late without ... you know that thing we're not supposed to say out loud."

Eleanor meant a crime wave or a case that needed solving. We have vowed to never say it out loud. I didn't need to be accused of swaying the pendulum in the wrong direction.

"Let's pay Bernice a visit. She might be a good candidate to adopt your kittens," Eleanor suggested.

I wrinkled my nose. "She has far too many mouths to feed in that department already. I certainly don't want to burden her with more."

Eleanor attempted to back her Cadillac from the garage, clunking the roof on the half-raised door. She threw open her door and inspected the damage, pointing her garage door opener at the door. It didn't budge.

"I think the door is caught on the car," I called out.

"Oh great. What do we do now?"

I stared up at the door in disbelief. This certainly wasn't the way I thought today would turn out.

"We might have to call a wrecker," I offered.

"Can't we just take your car today?"

I laughed. "I can barely get in and out of my car. Do you really feel up to it?"

"Let's give it a whirl."

Eleanor walked to my Mustang and squeezed into the vehicle with my help. I slid behind the steering wheel with a groan. "You don't look very comfortable, Eleanor."

"What makes you think that? Is it because my face is pressed against the windshield?"

"You need to move the seat back."

Eleanor fiddled in the front of the seat before she was able to move the seat back, but it didn't help her comfort an ounce. "I'll have to figure out something. This just won't do. Drive to Bernice's house and we'll worry about it later, but whatever you do don't get into an accident. It will take them two days to get us out of this tin can."

"What are you talking about? It might take two days for us to get out of the car when we get to Bernice's." I smiled.

I drove up Bernice's long and winding driveway. She lived in a rural part of Tawas City, the house concealed behind thick woods. Fewer branches slapped against my car as it was much smaller than Eleanor's Cadillac. It was then that I noticed the branches had been trimmed back since the last time we'd visited.

When the car skidded to a stop on the stone driveway I attempted to climb out of the car. Eleanor gave me a shove from the back and I narrowed my eyes at her after I picked myself up off the ground. I couldn't believe she propelled me that far with just one shove.

I smiled evilly at Eleanor when it was her turn to get out. "Do you need any help?"

"No, I don't!" Eleanor snapped. She worked her feet out of the car and grabbed the door and stood with a groan. "I did it," she proclaimed with a sweeping arm. She then rubbed her stomach. "You might want to call Andrew and ask him to switch cars with us. I don't think I can squeeze back into this car without internal damage."

"He's playing golf with the Hayes, but I'll try."

I called Andrew, who was indeed in the middle of eighteen holes. He promised to have someone else meet us.

Bernice had moved into this house last year. It was well kept for a time, but the weeds that now replaced the grass were knee deep. It always unsettled me whenever I walked through weeds. Burrs had a way of settling on my clothing.

We climbed the stairs of the porch and stared down at five cats. Forget about the cuddly sweet cats that most people might have, Bernice's cats are feral. The tiger cat howled and more cats packed the porch as if it was a battle cry and we were the foe. The yellow of the cats' eyes never left us and Eleanor hugged me tightly in fright. I didn't mind on this occasion, as I was just as frightened.

"Bernice!" I yelled praying she was within earshot.

The cats advanced and Eleanor and I were about to take flight when Bernice opened the door.

"Hello, girls," she greeted.

"C-Can you call off your c-cats?" Eleanor asked as she squeezed my arm tightly.

"Ain't no sense in trying to do that. Come on inside," Bernice said.

Eleanor and I moved together toward the door. The cats seemed to understand that we weren't to be eaten, so they backed off and allowed us inside.

"Whew, I thought we were goners," Eleanor exclaimed as she fell on the couch. She then wiggled and pulled out scissors. "Is there a reason you keep scissors on the couch?"

"Good you found them. I've been looking for them all week."

The wood floor of the house squeaked when I walked across it and settled in a brown recliner. It was the only furniture in the living room aside from the couch and one end table.

"Where did all your furniture go?" I had to ask.

"They went out with my fancy clothing," Bernice said.

I wasn't sure I should remark on the men's clothing Bernice was back to wearing.

"So that's why you're wearing men's clothing again. You got rid of your new clothing?"

Bernice pulled out a pipe and lighted it. "I donated them to the Salvation Army because I don't have further use for them."

I frowned as I took that in. Whatever did she mean she had no further use for them?

"Is there something going on that we should be concerned with?" I asked.

"Agnes is right. This is an unexpected turn of events," Eleanor said.

"I hardly call it a turn of events," I said. "Is there a reason for the abrupt change?"

Bernice sighed as she sat next to Eleanor on the couch. "It just wasn't me. At the time I thought it would make me happy. I was more well-dressed than even Elsie Bradford."

Elsie Bradford thought herself the social icon of Tawas, and one of our good friends, even though we didn't care much for her beau Jack Winston.

"Don't remind me. She had a fit about it," Eleanor said.

Bernice was lost in thought. I hated to break into her reverie, but I had to. "This doesn't have anything to do with your ex-husband Wilber, does it?"

Bernice jumped to her feet and began to pace. "I thought I could ... oh never mind."

"And here I thought you were getting along so well," Eleanor said. "He was here maintaining your yard."

I swallowed the lump in my throat. He certainly wasn't doing that any longer.

"Wilber hasn't changed a bit. He's the same roving-eyed man I was married to. I should have remembered he's a cheating louse."

Those were strong words for Bernice. "What happened?" I asked.

"Oh, I don't know. He just quit coming around."

"Did he say why?"

"No explanation or phone calls. He must have taken up with another woman." Bernice frowned. "Not that we were ever together like that now."

"So yard work was the extent of it?" Eleanor asked.

"That and a few dinners."

"So he just dropped out of sight?" Eleanor asked.

"Yup. Wilber was always a coward."

"Did you at least call him?" I asked.

Bernice folded her arms. "No reason to really."

"How long ago was this?"

"Couple of weeks."

"It's no wonder your weeds are out of control," Eleanor gasped.

"Eleanor!"

"At this point I can't be offended. I haven't seen Wilber for at least two whole weeks. He quit doing yard work months ago."

"Was he acting strange?" Eleanor asked.

"He was distracted whenever he came over, but he never mentioned anything."

"This is troubling," I said. "Have you heard from your children lately?"

"Callie and Angelo have their own lives. They don't want to be bothered by me."

"That doesn't sound right," I said. "I thought you had all reconnected."

"We tried, but unfortunately my children still harbor hard feelings about me. They live in Troy. There are more jobs down there," Bernice explained.

I frowned. "I'm really sorry that things didn't work out for you."

"I'm fine about it," Bernice said when she sat back down. "So what brings you girls by?"

"We're bored," Eleanor said. "It's been so quiet of late."

"Which is a good thing, because no crimes have been reported lately," I said.

Bernice interlaced her fingers. "Crime might take a rest, but it never retires."

"I suppose you're right. When is the last time you left the house?" Eleanor asked.

"It's been a few weeks, why?"

"You should come with us today," I said. "We could pay Rosa Lee Hill a visit."

"Maybe another day," Bernice said as she pulled on her pipe. "I'd much rather stay home and watch the deer and birds out my patio door. Did I tell you I had five coyotes in my backyard just yesterday?"

"That's scary," Eleanor said. "I must admit you have the perfect backyard for watching wildlife. Have you spotted any wild turkeys lately?"

"Nope. I hope those coyotes haven't eaten them all."

"I wouldn't worry," I said. "I imagine they haven't been taking their young for a walk just yet."

Bernice's laugh sounded more like a cackle. "You might be right. I hope you don't mind, but I have to feed my cats."

I shuddered, "That's all you needed to say."

CHAPTER 2

Martha, my daughter, stood next to her seventies paneled station wagon, dangling her car keys, when Eleanor and I returned to my car.

I reluctantly handed my keys to Martha.

"You'd better be careful," Eleanor said. "I'd rather not listen to her griping about you scratching her car."

"Whatever," Martha said with a careful pat of her teased-out blond hair. Today she wore a blue and black cat suit, her preferred mode of dress. Martha makes jewelry that she sells online, and the entire town had helped out at one time or another. She recently procured a distributor, but still makes one-of-a-kind jewelry.

I took Martha's keys and she jumped into my Mustang and tore off down the driveway before Eleanor and I even had time to get into the station wagon. I had a bad feeling about Martha using my car, but the wagon was much roomier.

Eleanor ejected an eight-track tape and popped in another one. It was a slow mode country tape that I had to remove before it got on my last nerve.

I headed back to town. "What do you think about Wilber's disappearance, Eleanor?"

"Strange. I'm so disappointed for Bernice. I know Bernice still loves her ex-husband, even if he left her for another woman years ago."

"And don't forget he managed to get custody of the kids."

"Perhaps it's not strange at all. I've always wondered if Bernice would allow Wilber back into her life after so many years."

I pulled around and headed in the opposite direction. "I'm bothered by Wilber's sudden disappearance. Let's go to Wilber's place and find out what gives."

"And I'll give him a piece of my mind," Eleanor said with a curt nod.

"Providing that he's okay," I added quickly.

"Do you think something untoward happened to him?"

"It's possible."

"We'd better hurry then."

I PULLED INTO WILBER'S DRIVEWAY. FARMERS LIVE IN THE AREA AND passing an occasional tractor was a common occurrence.

Wilber's blue truck was parked in the driveway. The curtains were drawn as I knocked on the door, casting Eleanor a nervous glance. Eleanor tried to peer though the small space where the curtains hadn't met. "I can't see anything," she complained.

"Let's see if there's another window where we can see inside."

Eleanor and I walked around the house, but none of the windows were low enough to see into. We climbed the deck out back. The blinds had been pulled aside and we could see into the dining room. Dirty dishes sat on the table and the only light on was the fluorescent one over the kitchen sink. I always kept mine on too and recognized the familiar glow.

Eleanor tried the patio door and it easily slid open. "Should we go inside?"

"I don't know. Wilber might not be happy if we surprise him in the bedroom."

"Who said anything about the bedroom?" Eleanor said with a shake of her head.

I opened the door the remainder of the way because Eleanor already had her paws on the handle. "Wilber!" I called out, listening for a response.

Eleanor frowned. "He might be injured."

"Let's hope so … . I mean, I hope that's all it is."

I attempted to shoulder Eleanor ahead of me through the door. She grabbed my shirt and yanked me inside.

We pinched our noses at the foul odor. "It smells horrible in here," Eleanor said as we walked into the living room. There was a large brown stain in the middle of the yellow carpet.

I walked up the hallway and the smell got worse. I could even smell it with my nose pinched. It was hard to hold my breath. I used my shirt to open the only closed door at the end of the hall. Wilber's corpse lay on the bed! I swatted the flies away as I hurried outside and stumbled until I was far enough away from the house to breathe.

"That was horrible," I cried.

"We shouldn't have come here," Eleanor added, tears in her eyes. "How long do you think he's been dead?"

"I imagine two weeks. Bernice mentioned that was the last time she saw him."

Eleanor nodded as she called 911. We waited in the front yard for the cops to arrive.

Sirens screamed up the road and four cars piled into the driveway. I sighed when Sheriff Peterson and Trooper Bill Sales, who is married to my granddaughter Sophia, approached.

"What do we have here, ladies?" Peterson asked.

"Wilber is dead."

"You forgot to tell him that he's been dead for a few weeks," Eleanor said.

"Or that's what we think," I added. "Based on the foul smell."

"It's so horrible that it made my eyes water."

Peterson motioned his deputies toward the front door with guns drawn.

"I hardly think there's a need for firepower," I said. "The patio door is open."

"It was unlocked," Eleanor added. "I accidentally opened it."

"We came in because we thought he couldn't hear us knocking on the door."

"Do you usually do that when you come to someone's house?" Bill asked.

"I do when I come to do a wellness check."

"I don't know why you'd do a wellness check and not have the police do one," Peterson said. "You wouldn't like it if people thought you were breaking in."

"Who asked you to come here?" Bill asked as four officers walked out back.

I bit my lip. I didn't want to tell them who gave us an idea that Wilber might be in trouble, but I couldn't withhold information like that. "Bernice mentioned she hadn't seen Wilber for few weeks. She figured he didn't want to come over anymore."

"And we had to come over to check on him," Eleanor added. She shuddered. "I'm sorry I went inside. It was horrible."

"I think he's been dead for at least a few weeks."

"Oh, and are you a coroner?" Peterson asked, raising his bushy brows.

"No, but I've never seen a body in that condition."

"There's a large brown spot on the living room carpet," Eleanor added.

"But we found the body in the bedroom. I can't imagine why the culprit would move the body."

"Wait by my car," Peterson ordered.

Under ordinary circumstances I'd argue with him about us being kept away from the scene, but this time I'd much rather be upwind.

"Now we know why Bernice hasn't seen Wilber in two weeks," Eleanor said.

"But we still don't know who or why someone would kill Wilber."

"Bernice mentioned he was distracted of late."

"I wish he'd been more forthcoming with her. At least then we'd have an idea of who might want him dead."

"This is so awful," Eleanor said. "Bernice will be crushed."

"And his kids will be too. She mentioned they live in Troy."

"Do you think they might be responsible for their father's death?"

"We'll have to speak to them, but I can't imagine they'd want their own father dead."

"They're suspects at this point until they can be cleared," Eleanor said.

"I know, but I hate the thought of children murdering their own father."

"It happens all the time. Don't you watch the ID channel?"

"You know I do. Bernice is considered a suspect too at this point."

Eleanor's hands slipped to her hips. "You know Bernice didn't do this. She told us she hasn't seen him—."

"I know what she said, but we need to ask her a few questions. She might remember something important when she finds out Wilber was murdered."

"She'll be too shocked to question. And I hate to think one of our friends is a murder suspect."

"The cops always look at a spouse or ex when someone is murdered," I reminded Eleanor. "Standard procedure."

"We should tell the sheriff we're leaving, and then we can sneak over to Bernice's house."

"I'm with you on that."

Sheriff Peterson met us at his car with a handkerchief pressed against his nose. "You're right, I think Wilber has been there at least a few weeks. So, Bernice mentioned Wilber hadn't been by lately?"

"Yes. And we'd really like to give her the news. It might come easier from us."

"I can't allow you to do that. She's a potential suspect."

"We could go together," I suggested.

"Agnes is right. She'll need a friend. It will be a horrible shock to her," Eleanor said.

"Fine we'll leave in a few minutes. Sales can handle the scene until forensics arrives."

I drove back to Bernice's. This will break what's left of Bernice's fragile heart.

Eleanor knocked on Bernice's door and she opened the door, an orange cat in her arms. "I didn't expect you back," Bernice said. Her eyes then widened. "What is Sheriff Peterson doing here?"

"That's what we'd like to talk to you about," I said.

Bernice led the way inside and shooed the cats out the patio door. She returned to the living room, where Peterson somberly said, "Have a seat, Bernice."

"I'd rather stand," Bernice fired back.

"Please, Bernice, have a seat," I pleaded with her.

She threw up her arms as she sat down. "Happy now?"

"When was the last time you saw your ex-husband?" Peterson asked.

"Like I told Agnes and Eleanor, he hasn't come around for two weeks. Why?"

"Did you go to his house recently?"

"Nope. I figured Wilber found another woman to spend his time with. He's like that."

"Bernice," I began. "Eleanor and I found Wilber's body at his house."

Her eyes widened and the color left her tanned face. "Why would you go over there?"

"To check on him," I said. "I thought there might be a reason why you hadn't seen Wilber for a while." I stared at the floor. "I wish I hadn't found him like that, but we believe he's been dead for a few weeks."

Peterson said, "Bernice, I believe Wilber was murdered."

Bernice clambered to her feet. "That isn't possible! Nobody would want to hurt Wilber!"

I wanted to kick the sheriff when he asked, "Not even you?"

"I recently reconnected with Wilber. Why would I want him dead?"

"How angry were you when Wilber quit coming around?"

Eleanor put a finger in the air. "But sheriff, if he's been dead for a few weeks Bernice didn't have time to be angry with him."

"Bernice was hurt, not angry, when she spoke to us this morning about Wilber's absence."

"In my experience, I'd expect even an ex-wife to shed some tears when she finds out her ex has been murdered."

Bernice walked over to the sheriff. "If you looked around my place you'll see I've had a hard life. It's desensitized me, my doctor claims. I don't even cry at funerals." She wiped a hand across her face. "I feel really bad about Wilber. I can't imagine someone killing him. He's even-tempered and doesn't have a mean bone in his body."

"Then why did you get divorced?" Peterson asked.

"Sheriff!" I gasped.

"It's fine, Agnes. Wilber had an affair and left me for another woman. Satisfied?" She walked over and tipped a jug with a skull and crossbones on it and wiped her mouth. "I didn't kill him even when he got custody of my children, so I don't expect I'd kill him now. We're friends."

"Any romantic involvement?"

"I've had my thoughts, but no we've never gotten to that. Wilber's mind was elsewhere of late, but he didn't tell me why … and I'm not the sort to question him. I figured if he wanted me to know he'd tell me."

"Would you mind if I had a look around your house?" Peterson asked.

"I hope you don't have a cat allergy. They have the run of the place."

Eleanor and I stayed in the living room with Bernice while the sheriff opened the door to two deputies who assisted him with looking around the place.

"I'm so sorry, Bernice," Eleanor said. "I can't believe the sheriff would accuse you of being involved in Wilber's murder."

"Are you sure you don't know of anyone who might want to hurt Wilber?" I asked.

"Nope. Already told the sheriff that."

"How did he get along with your children?" Eleanor asked.

"Why you bringing them up?"

"It's likely that Peterson will be questioning them too."

Bernice gasped. "You can't let him do that. They would never harm Wilber!"

"We could touch base with them first if you'd like," I said. "No telling if the cops will give them the news tonight, but I'd imagine they might."

Bernice grabbed my shirt. "You can't let them do that. I should be the one to tell them."

"You shouldn't do that, Bernice. The sheriff already considers you a suspect. He'll want to question them."

"Unless we get their first," Eleanor said. "Agnes and I could leave right now if you give us their addresses."

Bernice rattled off the addresses and phone numbers. She squeezed my hands. "Please tell them gently, and please don't question them too hard. I know they'd never harm their father. They'll be devastated when they hear he's dead. Do you have to tell them he was murdered?"

"I'll have to. The cops will tell them."

"You should leave before the sheriff notices you're gone."

"He won't like this," Eleanor said as she tugged me out the door.

We piled into the station wagon and I turned around and left despite Peterson staring at us.

"Peterson will be gunning for us after this," I said.

"He'll have to find us first. I hope you plan on stopping at a drive-through before we leave. Troy is quite a ways from here."

CHAPTER 3

The traffic in Troy was horrible, and I clung to the steering wheel with a death grip. Forget about turning at the light, I had to use turnarounds that had their own traffic signals. I was so confused, and having so many fast-food restaurants and businesses blanketing the landscape didn't help.

"Are we lost?" Eleanor inquired.

"What do you think?"

Eleanor gripped her purse. "It was just a question. Maybe we should stop and ask for directions."

"I'm afraid I'll never get back into traffic if I do that. We should call Callie and Angelo before we drop by their houses."

"I can't imagine they'll be home. I bet they're still at work."

"I don't even know what they do for a living," I admitted.

"We should have asked Bernice."

"I have a feeling she wouldn't know."

"I think you're right. Bernice mentioned reconnecting with her children hadn't gone well."

"It will be interesting to hear what Bernice's children have to say," I said.

Eleanor and I nervously sat on the couch in Angelo's house. Bernice's daughter, Callie, helped her brother in the kitchen.

"What do you think they're doing?" I asked.

"Plotting our demise?" Eleanor shrugged.

Angelo and Callie walked into the room carrying four glasses of lemonade. They set them down on the table, and Eleanor and I each scooped one up and took a sip.

Callie's slight frame was spilled into a white business suit. She had blond hair, whereas Angelo had dark hair. The last time he was in Tawas he had a shaved head, but now he had a full head of hair. His shirt was unbuttoned nearly to his waist and I couldn't help but stare at the swatch of dark hair on his chest. It was rather distracting.

Callie cleared her throat. "You mentioned on the phone you needed to speak to us about our father?"

"Yes, that's right. When was the last time you spoke to him?" I asked.

"A few weeks ago when we were in Tawas," Angelo said, "Why?"

"Two weeks ago," Eleanor gasped.

I shot Eleanor a look and tried to smooth things over by saying, "Did you see your mother while you were in town?"

Angelo cleared his throat. "We haven't spoken to her in months," he admitted.

"No?" Eleanor asked. "I thought you had all reconnected."

"I'd rather not discuss this. It's a private family affair."

Callie plucked invisible lint from her skirt.

"You certainly seemed happy to see her again not long ago," I said.

"Even your father spent some time with her," Eleanor said.

"I don't know what you mean," Callie said. "Dad told us there was no reason to keep in contact with her."

"Why would he say that?" I asked.

"There was a reason she didn't have custody of us when we were children."

"She spent time in a mental ward," Angelo hissed.

"Most mothers would go off the deep end if they lost custody of their children," I said, "especially if her ex moved in the other woman so quickly."

"You both should be ashamed of yourselves judging your mother like this," Eleanor scolded. "Even if she was the worst mother in the world that doesn't mean she might not have changed."

"This is none of your business," Angelo exclaimed.

"So you paid your father a visit two weeks ago?" Eleanor asked. "Both of you?"

"Why does it matter?" Callie asked.

"Because we found your father's body earlier today," I said to their shocked faces.

"He's been dead for about two weeks," Eleanor added.

Tears rolled down Callie's cheeks. "He was fine when we were there."

"It's okay, Callie," Angelo said as he patted his sister's hand.

Eleanor glared at Bernice's children. "You must have at least observed something out of the ordinary when you visited him. How was his health?"

"He was fine," Callie cried.

"Your mother said he'd been distracted lately," I said.

"Probably because of her efforts to reconcile with him," Angelo said.

"Your father went to see your mother of his own accord. I don't understand your harsh opinion of your mother."

"You should probably come to Tawas," Eleanor said. "Sheriff Peterson will want to speak to you. And you'll have arrangements to make for your father."

Callie ran into the other room. Angelo stood up and threw open the front door. "We've heard enough. It's time for you to leave."

Eleanor and I walked to the door. "Are you sure this is how you want to handle things?" I asked.

"I'll make sure Sheriff Peterson is aware of my father's distrust of our mother. If anyone killed him, it's her," Angelo said from beneath hooded eyes.

"What did she do to make you think that?" I asked. "You're pretty quick to throw your mother under the bus," Eleanor said with a curt nod. When Eleanor and I walked outside Angelo slammed the door shut. "What's his problem?" Eleanor asked.

"I certainly don't understand the anger," I said.

"We did accuse them of murdering their father."

"We alluded to it. There's no way we could know for certain, but the time line is certainly interesting."

"And they both claimed to have been in town."

"We'll have to touch base with Sheriff Peterson when we get back."

Eleanor and I waited in Peterson's office. I had to suppress the urge to take a look in the file that was on his desk.

Boxes were stacked in the corner. Eleanor was peeking inside one when Peterson cleared his throat as he entered the room. "I need to fire whoever let you in my office."

"The door was open," I said.

"And you helped yourselves?"

"I was just curious what you have in the boxes," Eleanor huffed.

"I promise I didn't look at the file on your desk," I quickly added.

"How tempting was that?"

"Very, but I'm quite aware that we're on the edge with you as it is. I'd hate for you to shut us out of cases."

"We came here to share information," Eleanor volunteered.

Peterson plopped down in his chair that for once didn't squeak. He'd shed about forty pounds the past six months.

"Go ahead. I can't wait to hear what you have to say." He smiled.

Peterson's lips barely moved when he smiled and I felt he was mocking us.

"We paid Wilber and Bernice's children in Troy a visit."

"Troy, you say?" Peterson asked as he jotted that bit of information down. "I didn't get a chance to find them yet." He frowned. "Did you two blab about Wilber's death?"

"You don't have to be rude," Eleanor said. "We're trying to help."

"And now we've lost the edge when we do speak with them. I hope you didn't accuse them of killing their father."

"Well... ." I began. "Angelo told us they were in Tawas a few weeks ago."

"Both of them?"

"Yes. But they denied having anything to do with Wilber's death."

"Angelo was too busy throwing Bernice under the bus," Eleanor said.

I cued the sheriff in about Angelo's thoughts about his mother and her past.

"Wilber did come to see Bernice," Eleanor reminded the sheriff.

"I'm aware of that. I'm hoping Wilber's friends come forward about his movements the last month. I believe Bernice didn't have anything to do with his death, but keep that between us for now. I want her to think she's still a suspect."

"I imagine she still is. I don't blame you for that."

"We told Angelo and Callie that they should come to Tawas," Eleanor said. "They're aware that you'll want to question them."

"What bothers me the most about Angelo is that he said so many horrible things about his mother. It wasn't long ago that Bernice reconnected with her children and ex-husband," I said.

"We thought it was water under the bridge," Eleanor added. "It will crush Bernice when she learns what Angelo said about her."

"Then don't tell her," Peterson offered. "It would be easier for her to not know."

"I can't keep that from her, not when Angelo will be in town soon. I don't want her shocked when he tells her how he feels about her possible role in Wilber's death."

"Fine, but I expect you to report back to me about her reaction."

"We'll be happy to. What can you tell us about Wilber's remains? Has a cause of death been determined yet?"

"How can I be sure that you'll keep this to yourselves?"

"You'll have to trust us," I said.

Peterson leaned back in his chair. "Sorry, but that's not good enough."

"We'll have to try harder," Eleanor said. "How about if we pinkie swear?"

I rolled my eyes at Eleanor. "I give you my word. We want to help solve this case."

"Wilber suffered a gunshot wound to his chest."

"I wonder why the killer moved his body to the bedroom."

"The killer didn't move him. Wilber was shot in his bed."

"What about the bloodstain on the floor in the living room?"

"That blood didn't belong to Wilber."

"So we have another victim?"

"It's possible. That or Wilber murdered someone."

"How can you be certain he was shot in bed?" Eleanor demanded.

"We found the bullet wedged in the mattress."

I sighed. "Bernice didn't say Wilber was seeing anyone. He was distracted."

"If Wilber killed someone that would make him very distracted," Eleanor pointed out. "I've only seen him at Bernice's house a few times, but he didn't seem the killing type."

"He was quite capable of demanding custody of the children when he divorced Bernice," I said and then gave the sheriff the details about the divorce.

"I'm not certain at this point if it's prudent to speak to Bernice again. She doesn't seem to know much about Wilber's recent movements," Peterson said.

"Let us know if Wilber's children ever show up in town."

I led the way back to the car and munched on the doughnut I'd snagged on our way out. It was always worth coming to the sheriff's department if we could reward ourselves with a sweet treat.

❦

BERNICE FROWNED AS SHE SAT OPPOSITE ELEANOR AND ME. SHE drummed her fingers on her abdomen nervously and said, "I just don't understand what I did wrong. It was great to speak to my children again, but it ended abruptly a few months back."

"Angelo spoke harshly of you. Callie didn't have anything to say."

"He's right about everything he said about me, but that was years ago, when he was only a child. He was only three when we broke up. Wilber and I kept our problems to ourselves."

"I don't think he has ever gotten over not having you in his life," Eleanor said.

"It's always a hard thing when your mother is gone," I agreed.

"He was so kind to me not long ago," Bernice mused. "He certainly changed his mind about me. I can't help but wonder why."

"Someone has to be involved here," Eleanor said. "Wilber must have been involved with someone else."

"Or had friends who didn't have a good word to say about Bernice." Eleanor fidgeted and pulled on her fingers. "He lives in the country. How will we be able to question his neighbors, Agnes?"

"We'll just have to knock on doors and see what we can find out. Hopefully we'll be able to track Wilber's movements. It might lead us to potential suspects."

"I wish I could help," Bernice said. "But I shouldn't be involved with the investigation because Peterson considers me a suspect."

I paced for a few moments. "Actually, I rather like the idea of you helping us with this case. We need to clear your good name and find out who in town is tarnishing it by bring up the past."

"Should I change clothes?"

"Whatever for?" Eleanor asked. "I don't see anything wrong with what you're wearing."

"But people will know who we are."

"They know who we are already."

"I mean me."

"Don't you dare change anything," I said. "I refuse to allow anyone to say a bad word about you. I can't believe that many people even know where you live."

"Or what your name is," Eleanor added. "Besides, it's not scandalous to have been divorced."

"You should know how rumors were back then, Eleanor, but I can't say any of those people still live in town or are even alive."

I tapped my foot. "Let's go ladies."

I drove west and coasted past Wilber's house. It had been boarded up and covered with crime scene tape. "Can you believe they boarded up the crime scene already?"

"They need to keep it secure."

"I wish we could go into Wilber's house," Bernice said. "How well did either of you examine the house?"

"That's one place you don't need to go," Eleanor said. "You don't need to see that."

"Especially that crime scene. Wilber has been dead for a few weeks," I said with a groan. "Please promise me you won't go there, Bernice."

"How would I get there when I don't have a car?"

"Whatever happened to that old truck you had?"

"Wilber sold it for scrap."

"You gave him permission to do that?" Eleanor asked. "Why?"

"It didn't run and it was too dangerous for my cats to climb around."

"Was it your idea to get rid of it?" I asked.

"Wilber mentioned it and I had to agree. There was no sense in keeping it around. If I didn't live in the woods someone might have complained."

"Since when has that ever happened in Tawas?"

"It depends on who does the complaining."

I slowed as I approached a driveway nearest to Wilber's, where a black truck with a lifter was parked.

CHAPTER 4

Bernice knocked on the door as Eleanor and I held back.

A man with red suspenders answered the door. "Cat Lady, is that you?"

"You can call me Bernice. Could we come inside and talk about my ex-husband Wilber?"

"Of course. Come on in."

We walked inside and were directed to the couch. The man sat opposite us. It was your typical man's house -- minimally furnished, huge flat-screen television. "I don't think I know your friends, Bernice," the man said.

"I'm Agnes and this is Eleanor. We're helping Bernice investigate a case." I didn't think it would hurt to lead him to believe Bernice was the reason we were here.

"I'm Robert Boyd," he said. "Does this have anything to do with all the cops at Wilber's house?"

"Do you know anything about that?" I asked.

"No." He frowned. "Is Wilber okay?"

"He's dead," Bernice muttered.

"Dead!" Robert gasped. "What happened?"

"I was hoping you could tell us," Eleanor said. "I mean, you're practically neighbors."

"I don't know Wilber that well. We spoke whenever I saw him in town, but that's the extent of it."

"Have you ever been at his place?" I asked.

"I hope the sheriff doesn't consider me a suspect. I've never been at Wilber's house."

"Can you tell us about his comings and goings? Just tell us anything you observed."

"I try to mind own business. I don't make a habit of spying on my neighbors."

"How about any lady friends who might have stopped by his place?" Bernice asked.

Robert pulled on his scruffy beard. "Sorry, I can't help you."

"Have you noticed any cars parked in the driveway of late?" I asked.

Robert fell silent for a time and then said, "Now that you mention it, a black SUV has been parked there a few times a week."

"When was the last time you saw it?" I asked.

"About a few weeks ago. It was about the same time Wilber began neglecting his lawn."

"And you didn't think to check on him?" Eleanor asked.

"I told you, I don't know him that well."

"Is there anything else you might have noticed?" Bernice asked. "It's really important."

"I wish I had checked on him."

"Did Wilber ever try to sell you an old truck?" I asked.

"You mean that rusted heap of junk he had? Jimmy towed it away."

Eleanor narrowed her eyes slightly. "I thought you only saw a black SUV there."

"So much for you not watching your neighbors. Did you see a woman over there?"

Robert backed up. "I never saw any woman there other than his daughter."

"Wilber's children paid him a visit a few weeks ago," I began.

"Now that I think about it, his son drives an SUV. It might have been him."

"Except that he couldn't have visited twice a week as you suggested because he lives and works in Troy."

"I don't know anything about that."

"That's convenient," I began, "whenever the questions become too tough you just say you don't know anything."

"We'll show ourselves out," Bernice said with a tight nod.

"Does Wilber or Callie own a black SUV, Bernice?"

"I haven't seen them in months."

"It might be someone else who has been going to Wilber's," I said.

"He found himself another woman. I should have known not to trust that man," Bernice grumbled.

"How was his health?" Eleanor asked.

"Good enough I suppose, why?"

"It could have been a visiting nurse," I suggested. "He might not have wanted to tell you he had medical problems."

"But it makes no sense when it comes to his murder," Eleanor said. "I suppose we're going to the impound yard now."

"Why?" Bernice asked.

"I was hoping that Jimmy would remember any strange goings on," I said.

THE DRIVE TO THE TOW COMPANY WAS A QUIET ONE, EACH OF US digesting the information dealt to us. So far a black SUV was our only clue -- and not much of one -- but it was all we had at the moment. I still wondered whose blood was on Wilber's carpet. It was certainly too much for the victim to get off the floor without help. I'd have to ask Peterson if he'd checked for any 911 calls from Wilber's address.

Jimmy was coming out of the office when we pulled up. Bernice waved at our approach. "Nice seeing you, Jimmy," Bernice said as she was the first one out of the car.

Jimmy curtly nodded at Bernice. "I heard about Wilber. How are you doing, Bernice?"

"Resolved to find out who done him in."

"What have you ladies found out?"

"We're still investigating. One of his neighbors mentioned seeing you towing Bernice's old truck from Wilber's house," I said.

"Yup. Wilber wanted to scrap it, so I gave him a hand. It's a shame it's so rusted out. I would have loved to restore it."

"That old truck?" Bernice asked.

"How long have you had it?" I asked.

"I picked it up cheap years ago."

"It's a 1955 Studebaker," Jimmy explained. "I didn't scrap it yet. I took it to my brother's house while I think about it."

"I'd love to see it restored," Bernice said.

"Let's get back to Wilber," I said. "Did you happen to notice anyone at Wilber's place when you came to check out the truck?"

Jimmy frowned. "I didn't see another woman over there, if that's what you mean ... or now that I think about it — Faith Fleur's vehicle was parked over there a few times I drove past."

"What kind of car does she drive?" Bernice asked.

"Black Equinox. It's a really sharp ride. But I hardly think she was at Wilber's place for the reason you might think, Bernice. She's too young, mid-twenties I believe."

"Where would we be able to find Faith?" I asked.

"Faith is Rosa Lee Hill's boarder."

"Rosa Lee is renting rooms?" I asked.

"That's what Curt and Cutis told me. Those boys have been having a spitting contest over the woman."

"I can't see Rosa Lee putting up with that," I said.

"Can't tell you nothing about that. You'll see for yourselves when you drop by. Try not to jump to conclusions."

"Who, us?" Eleanor asked with a shocked expression. "We never do."

I drove home in silence to the tune of my growling stomach and pulled in behind Andrew.

"It's getting a little late for investigating tonight," I said on the way inside.

Andrew was eating a slice of pizza.

"You ordered pizza! How thoughtful."

"I figured if I wanted to eat I had to." Andrew smiled. "Hello Bernice. We have plenty of pizza."

"I'm not hungry," she said sadly. Her eyes lit up when she spotted the kittens. "You didn't tell me Duchess had kittens!"

"Don't try to pick one up. Duchess has clawed all of us when we've tried."

Bernice gently picked up a black ball of fur, Duchess looking on protectively.

"What beautiful kittens you have, Duchess," Bernice said as she nuzzled the kitten and put it back down.

"I can't believe it," Andrew said. "She hasn't allowed us near her kittens."

"Well, I am the Cat Lady." Bernice grinned.

I turned to Andrew and grabbed a slice of pizza. "I thought you might want to know that —."

"There's a crime spree in Tawas?" he interjected.

I cast Bernice a sympathetic glance as she sat heavily in the kitchen. "My ex-husband is dead," she muttered. "I still can't believe it."

Andrew's eyes widened and he took hold of her hand. "I'm so sorry. What happened?"

"We don't exactly know," I said. I then brought Andrew up to speed about finding the body.

"That must have been horrible."

"I'm sure glad I wasn't there," Bernice said. "I feel so responsible for not calling someone to check on Wilber."

"You're not responsible for anything," Eleanor said. "You didn't kill the man."

I nodded as I grabbed soft drinks from the refrigerator and handed them out. "Eleanor is right. We have to find out who killed Wilber in his own bed."

"Don't forget about the other victim."

Andrew's brows furrowed. "Other victim?"

"Yes. There was a bloodstain in the living room, and it wasn't Wilber's."

"I can't imagine Wilber would kill anyone," Bernice said.

"I agree," I said. "And he never mentioned that he was seeing anyone."

"Maybe he didn't want to tell Bernice. It makes sense," Eleanor said. "But what did you talk about when you saw him?"

"We talked about our children. I was happy to see them after all these years, but they'd become distant. Wilber didn't understand it, but he didn't want to get involved because they're adults."

"That's hardly fair. He's the reason you never saw them all those years," I said. "They certainly seemed to harbor bad feelings about you. I can't help but wonder why when they initially received you back into their lives."

"What did Wilber do in his spare time?" Eleanor asked.

"He didn't really say."

"Are you hiding something from us?"

"Eleanor, stop harassing Bernice," I chided.

"I'm not. It's just that Wilber must have talked about more than just their children."

"He cut my grass and we chatted idly about what's happening in town."

"And what did you tell him?"

"That they're having a book sale at the library. Oh, and Elsie is planning a rummage sale."

"Are you sure about that? That doesn't seem like something Elsie would do," I said.

"What was the last thing you talked about?" Andrew asked.

"I already told you," Bernice said.

"It's about time we have something more to go on for tomorrow," I said.

"But I thought we could do it today," Eleanor said.

"It's getting too late for that, and I must admit I'm tired."

Bernice's bottom lip protruded slightly. "But I thought we were going to question that floozy."

"Now let's be fair. We don't know if the woman is a floozy yet," I said.

"You heard what Jimmy said. That woman was seen at his house a few times a week."

"Were you in a relationship with Wilber?" Andrew asked.

"No, but that doesn't mean that woman didn't have anything to do with Wilber's death."

"I'm sorry. I know this is hard for you, but Agnes and Eleanor will find out who murdered Wilber. You can sleep in the spare bedroom tonight."

"Spare bedroom," Eleanor gasped. "Whenever I've stayed over I slept on the couch."

"That could be because that's where you passed out," I joked.

Eleanor's hands slipped to her hips. "I'll have you know that I don't drink! Except when we're at one of Elsie's card parties. And I always go home, unlike someone I know who falls asleep in the parking lot of the One Stop."

"That's enough," Andrew cautioned. "Bernice didn't come here to listen to you two argue."

"I only passed out in my car once at One Stop, but that was before I was involved with Andrew," I told Eleanor.

"You're right. I don't know why I brought that up," Eleanor sighed.

"Are you done arguing already?" Bernice asked. "It was taking my mind off my troubles."

"I'll get the guest room ready," Andrew said.

"Don't bother, Agnes will run me home."

"Are you sure you want to be alone tonight?"

"I've been alone a good spell of my life. And I have my cats to keep me company. I really need to get home to feed them."

I drove Bernice home in silence. My right eye twitched as I focused on the road. I hated to drive at dark and wished I hadn't dropped Eleanor off so I'd have someone to talk to. Bernice said nothing. I felt bad that she was alone, although she did have her cats for company. I thought she and Wilber were a couple and it bothered me more than I could say. Wilber hadn't treated Bernice as she deserved. And her children were just as bad. I would certainly have trouble keeping my anger at bay when Angelo and Callie rolled into town.

CHAPTER 5

"Why do you have Martha's station wagon?" Andrew asked as he walked me outside the next morning.

"Eleanor and I don't exactly fit in my Mustang." I frowned. "We felt like sardines."

Andrew laughed. "Thanks for the visual."

"Martha agreed to exchange vehicles with me."

"Hmm. I can see Martha zooming up and down U.S. 23 as we speak."

"I was thinking that I really should let the car go and sell it."

"Sell your Mustang?" Andrew asked in shock. "You love that car."

"I did, but I need a car that's comfortable for Eleanor and me. It was an impulse buy, to be honest."

"That's what I like about you; you're spontaneous."

"I have to be when it comes to investigating."

"Why would you take your Mustang yesterday?"

"Because you had your SUV."

"I meant, is there someone wrong with Eleanor's Cadillac."

"She got it stuck in in her garage; something to do with the garage door."

"I'd better go over there and fix it."

"I had no idea you were so handy." I grinned.

"If I can't figure it out I'll give Jimmy a call."

"You should call him before you get there."

"Don't worry, I have it handled. Do you want to take my LX today?"

"No. I don't really mind Martha's car, even though it only takes eight tracks and the radio only brings in static."

"At least now you look your age. I mean when you get out of the car."

"Stop while you're behind. I know what you meant. Sort of."

"It's just that you're as vintage as the car."

I pointed to my mouth and Andrew gave me a quick peck before I drove off. I smiled whenever I thought about my husband. I was fortunate to have him in my life, and Eleanor had her Mr. Wilson. It's one of the reasons Eleanor and I relate so well. Both of us married quite late in life. I laughed to myself.

I headed to the campground where Martha lives in my Winnebago. Martha, in short shorts and a crop top, was waxing my Mustang.

"I see you're taking care of my Mustang," I said.

Martha smiled. "It's the least I can do, but my station wagon looks the same way it did yesterday."

"That might be because it's so bleached out nothing can improve it. I'd also call it a heap of junk, but it handles wonderfully for a being a seventies model."

"Does that mean I can drive your Mustang for a while?"

Martha's toothy grin didn't sway me a bit. "That's why I came here. I'd be happy to keep driving your car while I handle the case I'm on, but don't get too comfortable driving my car. I think I might sell it soon."

"Why would you get rid of a car like this?" Martha asked.

"I hate to say it, but I think I'm too old for the Mustang. It doesn't fit me anymore or my aching hip and knees."

"I'd love to buy your Mustang."

"I'll give it some thought and tell you when I make my decision, but for now drive carefully."

"As you can see, I'm already taking good care of it."

"Which is the only reason you can still use my car."

"So what was happening at Bernice's house?"

I filled Martha in about the recent developments. "I have a mind to tell Bernice's children off. She doesn't deserve to be treated like that," Martha said.

I sat on the picnic table. "When you came to town I wasn't sure I wanted to have anything to do with you either."

"I remember you didn't even want me to stay with you."

"We hadn't spoken in years. I didn't even know you had gotten a divorce, or that you were globetrotting."

"I'm sorry about that. But we did reconnect in a good way. You even offered me a place to stay in your camper."

"It's not like I let you move into my house."

"And I wouldn't want to live there. I love the beach. It's so inspiring that I began my jewelry business here."

"How is that going?"

"Great. And I have so much less stress now that I don't have to ask the Girl Scouts or senior citizens to help me keep afloat."

"It turned into a community effort. I applaud your tenacity, Martha."

Martha hugged me and gushed, "Thank you, Mother!"

"I don't suppose you can check on Bernice for me? I have a few things I need to do before I pick her up. I don't want her thinking I've forgotten all about her, especially after what happened yesterday."

"You can count on me."

I picked up Eleanor and we drove to the sheriff's department. I greeted the woman in the dispatch manager's office. "Hello. I was wondering who we could talk to about the 911 call history of a specific address."

The woman shook her head. "We can't help you."

"But it's important," Eleanor said. "We're investigating an important case."

"You'll have to speak to the sheriff, but I don't think he'll tell you anything."

"Surely you must have heard about us. I'm Agnes Barton and this is my partner Eleanor Mason. We're investigators in town."

"Never heard of you."

A thin, dark-haired woman walked in and the receptionist waved her over. "Have you ever heard of a Agnes and Eleanor? They claim to be investigators."

"Hello ladies. How can I be of help?"

"They want a 911 call history. I told them we don't give out that information and to speak to the sheriff."

"Come into my office," the woman said.

Eleanor and I walked into the small office that had only a small desk for her computer and two chairs.

"I know it's a stretch, but we wanted to know if a 911 call has ever come from Wilber Riley's address."

"What's the number?"

I gave Bernice a quick call and she rattled off Wilber's number for me, which I then told the manager helping us.

She tapped the keys of her computer for a time before saying, "No calls from that number."

"So you can't tell us if the police were called to his address?"

"Sorry I couldn't be more helpful. Sheriff Peterson says so many wonderful things about you both. That's the only reason I checked the logs for you."

"We appreciate it. I don't want to bother the sheriff with this."

"I hope this helps you with your case."

"We were just wondering if our victim ever reached out to 911."

"You've been most helpful," Eleanor added.

Sheriff Peterson stopped us as we were ready to open the door leading outside. "What are you two doing here?"

Eleanor and I stared at one another. "We were just wondering if Angelo and Callie Riley arrived in town yet."

"They'll be here shortly. Angelo told me they were stopping at their mother's house first," Peterson said.

"Thanks, Peterson," I called out, and Eleanor and I hurried out the door.

"They better not have hurt Bernice," Eleanor said. "I have a mind to pop them in the mouth."

"At least Angelo, the jury is still out about Callie."

I floored it through town, which was free of tourists for the moment, and pulled up Bernice's driveway.

I raced to her door and shouldered my way inside to the sound of raised voices. And when we spotted Bernice on the floor, Eleanor's fists flew into action. She popped Angelo in the mouth and he dropped to the floor.

"What did you do to Bernice?" I demanded as I checked her pulse while Eleanor called 911. "I'm glad the sheriff told us you were coming over here."

Angelo rubbed his jaw and choked out, "I didn't do anything to Bernice. She was like that when we arrived."

Callie, pale, backed up with her arms in front of her, potentially to ward off Eleanor. "I didn't do anything, I swear."

Eleanor rubbed her fist and Angelo stepped quickly toward the door. "I think we should leave."

"I'm not going anywhere," Callie said as she knelt next to Bernice. "Mother, are you okay?"

"She isn't our mother," Angelo spat as he hurried out the door before any of us could stop him.

The sound of sirens had me scrambling toward the door. I watched in satisfaction as Trooper Sales walked Angelo back inside.

"So much for your great escape," I said, then nodded at Bill. "I didn't expect you to answer the call."

Two paramedics hurried in the door and began to assess Bernice.

"What really happened here, Callie?" I demanded. "Bernice wasn't on the floor when you arrived. I spoke to her not even ten minutes ago on the phone."

"Don't tell her anything, Callie," Angelo hissed.

"What's happening here?" Bill asked.

"When Sheriff Peterson told me Bernice's children were here I knew we had better get here fast," I gasped. "Angelo and Callie were standing over her. Bernice was sprawled out on the floor!"

Angelo waved his arms around as he said, "I have no reason to hurt Bernice."

"You should call her 'mom.' She gave birth to you," Eleanor ordered.

"She struck me," Angelo complained as he pointed a finger in Eleanor's face.

I shrugged. "I don't remember seeing anyone hit you. I was too concerned about Bernice on the floor."

"Two more first-responders came into the door with a stretcher and attended to Bernice. Her gray skin had dread creeping up my back. "Is she going to be okay," I asked.

"We need to get her to the hospital," one of the emergency workers said.

Eleanor and I hugged each other and looked on helplessly as our friend was hauled onto an gurney and carried to the ambulance.

"Why would you do this to your mother?" I demanded.

"What condition was Bernice in when you arrived?" Bill asked.

"She was on the floor when we arrived," Angelo said.

"Then how did you get in the house?" Eleanor asked. "Or get past her cats?"

"I kicked them out of my way."

"I oughta give you a kick," Eleanor hissed. "Animal cruelty isn't tolerated around here."

"What do you have to say?" Bill asked Callie. "Is he right? Was Bernice on the floor when you arrived?"

She looked at the floor and shrugged. "Angelo was the first in the door. I waited outside."

"See? She wasn't even in here!" Angelo yelled.

"If you don't shut up and let her talk … ," I threatened.

"I heard Angelo yelling," Callie admitted.

"We heard arguing when we arrived," I said. "Admit it, you attacked your own mother."

"She killed my father," Angelo insisted. "Our father!"

"Bernice would never hurt Wilber. She was still in love with him," Eleanor said. "And she doesn't even own a car."

"She had a truck."

"A non-running truck," I said as I turned to Bill. "Wilber sold Bernice's truck for her. You can verify that with Jimmy."

"I think we all need to go the sheriff's department where we can sort this out," Bill said. "I'll need to cuff the two of you because you're riding with me."

All the color left Callie's face. "Handcuff us?"

"I can't very well have you in the back of my car without cuffing you. It's a short drive to the sheriff's department."

"I heard my brother yelling at our mother," Callie gasped.

"Shut up, Callie! Don't act so innocent. We both wanted to confront her about dad."

"Not like that I didn't!"

"I have no idea who's lying," I said. "I'll meet you at the sheriff's department, Bill."

I took a peek under the porch, where Bernice's cats were huddled together. It was almost as if they understood their mistress and protector had left the house in serious condition.

"We need to check on Bernice," Eleanor exclaimed as I drove to the sheriff's department.

"It will take them time to assess her. Don't you want to be there to explain to the sheriff what happened here?"

"I don't know what happened. Trooper Sales will be able to tell the sheriff what happened. Bernice needs us at the hospital, she doesn't have anyone else."

"You're right. We can talk the sheriff later."

I pulled up to the hospital just as the EMS crew unloaded our friend and rushed her inside. We felt helpless. All we could do was tell the receptionist we were here for Bernice.

Eleanor and I plopped down in chairs and I grabbed a tissue for each of us. I couldn't control the tears. If only I had picked Eleanor up earlier and arrived at Bernice's house before her awful children arrived. I didn't need to be told that Angelo was the cause of Bernice's condition. I knew he was. We had to speak to Callie alone more now than ever. They hopefully said enough in front of Trooper Sales that Peterson would hold Angelo and Callie.

I picked up a magazine and flopped it back down after indiscriminately flipping through the pages.

"We should make some calls," Eleanor suggested. "Our friends will be so upset if we don't let them know what's happened."

"I think we should wait until we know her condition."

"We're not waiting. Bernice might be critical and she might die." Eleanor cried, and I wrapped my arm around her.

"We can't think like that. We have to be strong for Bernice." I pulled my phone from my pocket. "I'll call Rosa Lee and Martha. You should call Elsie and Marjory."

I called Andrew first to give him a heads up on what was happening and let him know that we planned to stay at the hospital.

CHAPTER 6

Eleanor and I hugged each of our friends as they arrived. Elsie and Marjory wouldn't let Eleanor or me go as we group hugged.

Both Elsie's beau Jack and Marjory's husband Bill came with her and helped pull Marjory and Elsie back before they smothered us.

Rosa Lee and her boys, Curt and Curtis, arrived with their game faces on. I knew in a pinch that Curt and Curtis would take Angelo out if we asked, though I never believed them capable of murder.

"Do you have any idea what happened?" Andrew asked when he walked into the lobby with Mr. Wilson.

"All we know for certain is that Bernice was on the floor when we arrived at her house," I said. "And Bernice's children were arguing with her. We heard arguing before we even walked in the door. They were trying to come up with a believable story about Bernice's condition, if you ask me."

"They didn't need to accuse her of murdering their father," Eleanor said.

"What?" Elsie gasped. "What didn't you tell us?"

"We found Bernice's ex-husband's body."

"He'd been dead for two weeks," Eleanor added.

"How horrible for Bernice," Elsie said. "I really hoped they would get back together."

"Not according to Bernice."

"Is it possible whoever killed Wilber might have tried to murder Bernice?" Marjory asked.

"Only if it's her children."

"Are you certain what happened to Bernice had something to do with her children?" Andrew asked.

"Eleanor and I think her condition has everything to do with them. Who would come to Bernice's to try to off her? She keeps a shotgun close at all times."

"Always liked Bernice," Curt said with a nod.

"Bernice doesn't know who murdered Wilber, and we've been working the case. We don't have much to go on." I didn't want to go in-depth about what we still planned to look into. Right now we had to focus on Bernice. I hated to think that she might die.

I glanced up as my granddaughter Sophia walked over to us dressed in her nurse's garb. "Dr. Thomas told me to bring you into a conference room. It will be more comfortable, and I've ordered a beverage and snack cart."

"Can you tell us anything?" I asked Sophia.

She sadly shook her head as we followed her into the room off the emergency department. The room had a large oval table with comfy chairs. Leather couches line two walls, and a cart contained pitchers of water, coffee and tea. Eleanor poured the coffee and I passed the basket of wrapped crackers and cookies around.

Andrew enfolded me into his arms and I sniffled as the tears slipped to the shoulder of his shirt. "I won't be able to deal with it if Bernice isn't okay. I blame myself for not getting there earlier."

Andrew pulled me an arm's distance away. "It's not your fault. You were trying to help her."

"We should have demanded she spend the night."

"We offered, but it was her decision to leave. She wanted to get back to her cats."

"That's just like Bernice to think about those cats of hers," Elsie said. "We don't call her Cat Lady for nothing."

"That name sure spread like a wildfire," Eleanor said, "but it never bothered her."

"Has she always lived like that?" Andrew asked. "Didn't she have her other house remodeled because someone wanted to use her property."

"Yes, but she told us she was more comfortable living much simpler," Eleanor said.

"It wasn't long ago she was dressing better than me," Elsie exclaimed with a smile.

"And did you ever get angry," Marjory reminisced.

"Not for long," Rosa Lee said. "Bernice told me it just wasn't for her."

"She told us the same," I said. "Wearing men's clothing fits her much better."

"I can't help but wonder if she changed because Wilber was coming around," Eleanor said sadly. "Us women will do anything when it comes to a man."

"You've never changed anything," Mr. Wilson said with a glint in his eye.

"Not true," I said. "Eleanor might not have changed where she lives or the clothing she wears, but she doesn't get into fistfights anymore."

Eleanor nodded. "I don't chase after men either."

"In your dreams, Eleanor," I said.

"You know, Bernice used to make moonshine," Curtis said.

"Don't remind me," I gasped. "She almost killed me."

"She used to make good moonshine," Rosa Lee said. "I've been friends with her longer than anyone. I suppose folks think we're both a little odd." She shrugged.

"Unique is the word I'd use," I said. "If all of us were the same, what fun would that be? I'm glad that you don't grow pot anymore, though."

"I wish I had some now," Jack said dryly from where he was sitting. "What? I have a medical card."

"I don't know why. You don't smoke it," Elsie said. "At least you'd better not."

"Like I can get anything past you, dear."

I smiled as I filled a glass with ice water and sat down at the table. It was nice to remember all the crazy things we've done and our memories about Bernice.

We jumped up when Sophia popped into the room. "I didn't mean to scare anyone. I was checking to see how everyone was doing."

"Don't you have any news?" I pleaded with her.

"All I can tell you off the record," Sophia whispered, "is that Bernice is having an MRI."

Andrew had to glide me to a chair. "Why would she need a MRI?" I asked.

"I'm sorry, I can't tell you anything else. Dr. Thomas will be here just as soon as he has something to share," Sophia said as she slipped back out the door.

"You'd think your granddaughter would tell us something of use," Elsie grumbled.

"Don't blame Sophia," Rosa Lee said. "She's a nurse first. And there are laws that prevent her from blabbing – unlike some people I could mention."

"I didn't blab about anything," Eleanor whined.

"I wasn't talking about you, Eleanor."

"Let's all calm down. There's no sense in getting testy with each other. We're here for Bernice."

"I wonder if she knows we're here?" Marjory asked no one in particular.

"She will soon. And she'll tell us to go home," I said. Bernice isn't the sort of person who'd want anyone fussing over her, but it was about time she knew how much we all love her.

Andrew turned on the television in the corner of the room and flipped it to the Hallmark Channel. We settled down to watch I Love Lucy. We needed the diversion and the humor as we wiled away the hours.

I THUMPED MY HEAD ON THE TABLE WHEN THE DOOR OPENED AND

Dr. Thomas closed it behind him. His eyes were red-rimmed and bags found their way onto his handsome face.

He eased down at the table with a folder in front of him.

"I'm sorry it's taken so long, but I was waiting for the test results. Bernice had a TIA, what we call a mini-stroke."

We gasped. "Is she going to be okay?" I asked.

"We've moved her to a private room. Bernice is resting now, but I'll allow you up."

"Did she wake up after coming here?"

"Yes, but we've given her something to relax her for the MRI. I wouldn't expect her to stay awake more than a few minutes at a time."

"She just found out her ex-husband was murdered," I said.

"That might explain her unwillingness to answer my questions. I think she needs to know you're here for her. It might help comfort her."

"When will she be released?" Elsie asked.

"It won't be soon. We'll perform more tests to find out what might have caused the stroke."

"She argued with her children today," I said.

"That wouldn't cause a stroke. She might have a clot or blockage somewhere. That's my main concern right now."

"Thank you Dr. Thomas," I said.

We went to the third floor and entered Bernice's room. An intravenous drip was running into one arm, and blood pressure cuff was attached to her other. An oxygen tube was tucked under her nose.

A nurse entered and motioned us into the hallway.

"Why is Bernice on oxygen?" I asked.

"We want to make sure she doesn't have any breathing problems through the night."

"Is it okay if we're here?"

"She really needs her rest, but Dr. Thomas told me to expect you all. It's not very comfortable and we don't have many chairs. Families normally have two people stay here at a time. You could relieve one another. Bernice should be awake sometime in the morning."

"Eleanor and I will stay," I volunteered.

"Call me if anything changes or when Bernice wakes up in the morning," Rosa Lee said. "I'll call everyone after you contact me, Agnes."

Andrew squeezed my shoulder. "Are you sure you want to stay?"

"Yes. It's really important to me. We'll get back to investigating once I know Bernice will be okay."

Eleanor and I held hands as we stood at Bernice's bedside. Bernice had some color to her face now, and I pressed my hand against my mouth to stifle the chuckle at her snoring.

We tip-toed to recliner chairs, unlocked the wheels and moved them closer to the bed. I jumped at the loud clicking sound when I pressed my foot to lock the wheels. It sounded like a shotgun blast in this quiet room. The nurse brought us blankets and showed us how to recline the chairs.

I sighed and closed my eyes to the sound of the occasional inflation of Bernice's blood pressure cuff. The events of the day made it very easy to fall asleep.

※

Loud snoring woke me early the next morning. The racket came from Eleanor, whose arms were off the chair, the blanket piled between her legs.

"I don't know how you can sleep with the way she snores," Bernice said.

I yawned and pushed my chair closer to her bed. I moved to hold her hand, but she slid it away. I should have known that Bernice wasn't the sort who would want anyone holding her hand. Not everyone is touchy feely, not even me most times.

"I'm glad to see you awake," I said. "I was so worried when I saw you sprawled out on your floor," I sniffled, dabbing at unshed tears.

"When was that?"

"Yesterday."

"Dr. Thomas told me I had a stroke, but I'm feeling too fine for that."

"An MRI confirmed it."

"Oh, he told me that too, but I'm not the sort to lie around all day in a hospital bed."

"But if the doctor recommends —."

"Poppycock! I'm leaving today."

"He's still trying to figure out why you had the stroke."

"My children had my blood pressure on the rise." She frowned as she shook her head. "To accuse me of murdering their father. I know Sheriff Peterson might consider me a suspect, but my own children."

"So you remember what happened yesterday?"

"Arguing with my children is the last thing I remember."

"Well, at least none of your brain cells are damaged."

"You say the sweetest things, Agnes."

"Angelo was the only one of your children who had anything to say."

"Including denying he was the cause of your unconsciousness," Eleanor said from her chair as she tried to untangle the blankets.

"We heard him arguing when we walked up. Angelo claimed you were already out on the floor when they arrived."

"Don't let Callie fool you. She had her say too," Bernice said sternly.

"At what point did you pass out?" Eleanor asked.

"I don't remember that or anything else after. I was out the whole night?"

"Dr. Thomas gave you something to relax you. You must have remembered having those tests."

"It's a complete blank."

"You really need to rest until Dr. Thomas releases you," I said. "We'll be more effective investigators if we don't have to worry about you."

"Bill took Callie and Angelo to the sheriff's department for questioning," Eleanor said.

"That's something." Bernice yawned. "I'm more tired than I thought. I'll stay here until the doctor releases me, but you have to promise to look after my cats. The cat food is locked up in the barn."

"Don't worry about your cats, we'll take care of them," Eleanor said. "And we'll have to call Rosa Lee so she can let our friends know you woke up."

"Who did you call?"

"We were waiting for an update with Elsie, Marjory, Jack, Bill, Andrew and Mr. Wilson in the lobby of the emergency department."

"Don't forget Rosa Lee and her boys," Eleanor added.

"Why did you bother them?"

"Because they're your friends, all of our friends and they care about you."

"Even Agnes and I put the investigation on hold," Eleanor said.

"You shouldn't have done that. We need to find out who murdered Wilber. Did you ask Rosa Lee about her boarder?"

"Not yet. Yesterday we needed to be here for you. We're still committed to investigating. We'll pick up where we left off today."

"You do that. And keep Angelo and Callie away from me or the next time I won't be the one hitting the floor," Bernice threatened.

"Nothing would make me happier," I said. "I hope I won't have to use my secret weapon."

Eleanor put her fists up. "I'm ready to go when you say the word, Agnes."

It felt good to hear Bernice laugh, especially after last night when we thought we might lose her.

CHAPTER 7

Eleanor and I strutted into the sheriff's department ready to make certain Angelo and Callie were still in custody. I didn't know what I'd do if they had been turned loose.

We knocked on Peterson's office door. He motioned us inside as he finished a phone call.

"How is Bernice?" Peterson asked, placing the receiver back in its cradle.

"Dr. Thomas said it was a mini-stroke. I think it was brought on by Bernice's children accusing her of murdering their father," I said.

"Strokes are caused by a blockage or clot of some sort."

"Her children yelling at her didn't help."

"I hope they're behind bars," Eleanor said.

"They've been questioned, but I'm about ready to release them."

"After what they did to Bernice?"

"It's not a crime to argue with someone or accuse them of murder. If it was, you two would have been locked up a long time ago."

"Getting back to Wilber's murder, remember Angelo and Callie admitted to being in town two weeks ago," I said.

"I remember you telling me that. I'll be looking into their movements during that time frame. I honestly doubt they murdered their father."

"Children do more often these days."

"What would their motive be?"

I frowned. Okay so he had a point. "We don't know yet, but we'll certainly find out if they would profit financially from his death."

"They both have good jobs in Troy," Peterson countered.

"What if they planned to frame Bernice? It's no secret they didn't wish to be involved in her life."

"That's a stretch, but I'll keep that under consideration."

"Bernice expressed that she doesn't want her children near her."

"And Dr. Thomas plans to keep her in the hospital," Eleanor added.

"I'll make certain they stay clear of Bernice," Peterson said.

"Will you be making them stay in town for the duration of the investigation?" I asked.

"I can't hold them much longer without charging them."

"Their father just died. Wouldn't they stick around to plan the funeral?"

"And they'll have to handle their father's estate, providing he had a will," Eleanor added.

"I don't have a reason right now to keep them in Iosco County. But there are other ways to keep tabs on them."

"Did they have anything to say about Wilber's death other than that they think Bernice is the killer?"

"They don't think her capable of murder now, not after the way she passed out. Angelo realizes how fragile his mother is now. But personally I consider Bernice far from fragile."

Eleanor puffed up her chest. "But last night... ."

"Let them think she's fragile if it means they'll leave her alone," I interjected. "What did Angelo have to say about lying about Bernice's condition before he arrived? He said she was already laid out on the floor. Bernice remembers arguing with him before she passed out."

"I'm aware of that, but people get confused about events."

"Bernice was the only one harmed."

"Why are you defending Angelo, Peterson?" Eleanor asked, pushing her fists into the arms of her chair.

"I'm not, but I'm not at the point where I can single out a suspect. We don't know whose blood is on Wilber's floor or if we have another victim." Peterson leaned forward. "Do you really believe Angelo and Callie are responsible for their own father's death?"

"You have a point, but I hope you won't turn Bernice children loose yet. You'll be a fool if you do."

I walked to the door and Eleanor called to me to slow down, which I didn't do until I was at the car. "I expected more of Peterson," I said as I merged onto U.S. 23.

"He's just doing his job. It has no reflection on ours. Weren't you supposed to call Rosa Lee and give her an update about Bernice's condition?"

"We're going there now. I hope Faith Fleur is there."

That satisfied Eleanor. She gripped her purse and took to staring out the window. I struggled to roll down the window as it was hot as blazes in the station wagon. Air conditioning wasn't a standard option for cars in the seventies.

The trees and houses passed in a blur as I sped south, grumbling when I passed a car and found a state police cruiser ahead of me. He was going below the speed limit, and activated his flashers and pulled over a car. I smiled when I saw it was Trooper Sales. I nodded as we passed him.

I pulled into Rosa Lee's driveway and frowned when I didn't find a black SUV parked there.

Eleanor and I waved at Curt and Curtis, who were working on their truck. Rosa Lee's brows knitted as she held the screen door open for us. "I thought you were going to call."

"I thought we'd stop by instead," I said. "Bernice is awake and complaining about being stuck in the hospital."

"It sounds like she's back to her old self. I'd better call the girls."

Eleanor froze, her tongue practically hanging out as she stared at blueberries piled on the table. "I smell blueberry pie."

I wrinkled my nose. "I don't care for blueberries."

"What about blueberry muffins? Blueberry pancakes?"

"You win. Blueberries are good in muffins and pancakes."

Rosa Lee hung up the phone. "One piece of blueberry pie coming up for Eleanor," she announced. She cut the pie and slapped it on a plate and handed it off to Eleanor.

"Do you have any Cool Whip?" Eleanor asked.

"Yup." Rosa Lee slid the topping to Eleanor and wiped her fingers on a towel. "I suppose you're back to investigating."

"Bernice insisted that we get back to work."

"Wilber was the love of Bernice's life. I know she's never let anyone know that. She's never given any man a chance since they divorced."

"You mean Bernice has other men in her life."

Rosa Lee clucked her tongue. "Not the way you mean, but she's gotten her fair share of attention through the years. She wasn't always the Cat Lady, you know."

"You and Bernice have been friends for a long time," I said.

"We're very much alike, although if you ask Bernice she'll deny it. I volunteered at the hospital Bernice had been admitted to. She didn't have anything to go back to when she was released."

"You mean the mental hospital?" I asked.

"It wasn't a mental hospital, only a wing of the hospital that specialized in treating people having a crisis. Bernice had a nervous breakdown thanks to Wilber taking her children. But she never said a bad word about him. She wanted them to get back together."

"She must have been disappointed when that didn't happen," I said.

"Which is why I took her in for a time. My pa had a rundown house that he gave her to live in. We helped her fix it up real nice. My husband was alive back then."

"I've never heard you talk about your husband before."

"Not much to say, really. He died in a tractor accident, leaving me to raise my two boys on my own."

"You've done a good job of it," Eleanor said.

"They got themselves into trouble like many boys do, but I beat it into them if they strayed back to crime after they got out of prison that I'd take a switch to them."

"It's no wonder they toe the line with you," I said.

"Oh they have their foolish moments."

"Did you take in a boarder recently?"

"How'd you know about that?"

"Our investigation led us there," I said. "Faith Fleur was seen a couple times a week at Wilber's house."

"Jimmy saw her there when he towed away Bernice's old truck," Eleanor said.

"That's not the name the woman gave me," Rosa Lee said. "We should mosey out there and ask her if she lied to me." Rosa Lee frowned. "She'll have to go if she's not who she said. It's bad enough she's a distraction around here."

As we walked outside I said, "I don't see a black SUV here."

Rosa Lee stopped walking. "The girl doesn't have a vehicle. Curt and Curtis have been hauling her around. Boys, get over here. Miss Agnes and Miss Eleanor have a few questions for you."

Curt came out from under the hood of his truck rubbing his head. "Dang it, Mom, you made me hit my head," he complained.

"Oh, you poor thing," I said, receiving a look from Rosa Lee.

"You oughta watch what you're doing," Rosa Lee said. "Where is that girl?"

"What girl?"

"Do you need to cut me a willow switch?"

"She went for a walk in the woods with Curtis," he sighed.

"Then why did you say what girl?" Eleanor asked, tapping her foot.

"Ma don't like us paying the girl any attention."

Rosa Lee frowned. "You see what I'm talking about, a distraction."

"I don't suppose this girl has a name?" I asked.

"Course she got a name." Rosa Lee pointed to the willow tree. "Her name is Gia Swanson. She's a real sophisticated gal, and from New York City."

"What's she doing here then?" I asked. "And supposedly with no car?"

"She doesn't have a car, I swear," Curt proclaimed.

"That or she isn't parking her car here," Eleanor offered.

Curt rubbed grease off his chin with a rag. "Think what you want, but I'm telling you... ."

"Mind your manners, boy! I haven't forgotten about that willow switch yet."

"Where's the trail? Eleanor and I could use a walk in the woods."

Rosa Lee walked with us to the edge of the woods and pointed out the trail. "I best not go with you. I might have to whip Curtis if he's doing more than kissing that gal."

"Thanks for the warning," Eleanor said.

Eleanor and I linked arms to help one another over the ruts and dips in the trail. I breathed in the scent of pine, and the needle-covered ground gave slightly under my feet.

"I don't see Curtis," Eleanor said, swatting a mosquito.

"We've only gone fifty feet. I can't imagine Curtis would want to stick too close to home if he's walking with a pretty girl."

"Oh, what was I thinking?"

"You were thinking like an old woman who doesn't get asked to walk in the woods." I smiled.

"Curtis," I called out.

Eleanor elbowed me. "Why are you calling his name?"

"Because I don't want to catch him doing something Rosa Lee wouldn't approve of."

Eleanor laughed. "That's messed up. Rosa Lee must know her sons are not children."

"I know that, but she keeps them on a short leash."

"Too short, not that I'd ever tell her that."

We walked toward the remnants of a half collapsed cabin. On the other side, Curtis was picking flowers with a young woman with jet black hair.

"Hello Curtis?" I called out as Eleanor flapped her hand in greeting.

The flowers tumbled out of his hands, scattering to the ground. The color left his face to return in a blush. "What are you doing here, Miss Agnes and Miss Eleanor?"

"We're looking for you," I said.

"And here you are picking flowers. Not what I expected to find when a young man takes a girl for a walk," Eleanor smirked.

"He was helping me find a particular flower," Gia said.

I stared at the small purple flower. "You can't find a violet by yourself?" I asked. "There are plenty scattered in the woods."

"Leave them alone," Eleanor scolded me. "We're here to meet the boarder. I'm Eleanor and this is Agnes. We're friends of Rosa Lee's."

"I'm Gia Swanson." She threw up her arms in a cheerleader pose.

I rolled my eyes as Eleanor asked, "Where are you from?"

"New York City."

"What brings you to Tawas?"

"I'm on vacation. I love the area, so I thought I might as well stay for a while."

"How nice. Isn't that nice, Eleanor?" I asked.

"Yes, it's very nice indeed."

"How did you come to be staying at Rosa Lee's?"

"I asked a waitress at G's Pizzeria if she knew anyone who had a room to rent."

"Curt and me told her about the spare room at Ma's house and we brought her home with us," Curtis said.

"Why would you go with two strange men?" I asked. "They could have been creeps or ax murderers."

"I'm a good judge of character."

My eyes widened. "Why are you really in town?"

"I just told you, for vacation."

"How are bankrolling your visit."

"Miss Agnes, be nice," Curtis chided.

"I have money saved up. And I'm working at the Dairy Queen in town."

"At least she's not lazy," Eleanor said. "I don't remember seeing an extra car parked in the driveway."

"My car broke down when I arrived."

"What kind of car is it?"

"It's a Toyota Camry. It got towed."

I massaged my chin. "That's interesting. Your car broke down, and Curt and Curtis just brought you to their mother's house to rent a room. Curt and Curtis are good mechanics. Why not have one of them fix your car?"

Gia's brows gathered in thought. "It got towed."

"Curt and Curtis are friends with the tow truck driver. I imagine they could get your car."

"Why are you asking me so many questions?"

"Because there has been a murder in Tawas City, and you're a newcomer in town."

"She didn't murder anyone," Curtis said.

"You couldn't possibly know anything about this girl," I said. "I think we need to have a talk with Rosa Lee. Gia could have bought a tent and camped out while in town."

"Do you know a Wilber Riley?" Eleanor asked. "We found him murdered yesterday."

"Wilber's dead?" Curtis asked with widening eyes. "Does Cat Lady know?"

"Yes, Bernice knows," I said. "She's in the hospital over this fiasco."

"I feel awful. We'd better head back, Gia," Curtis said. "I need to help find the killer."

Eleanor and I walked back to the house, stopping to catch our breath. "What do you make of Gia?" I asked.

"I didn't believe one word out of her mouth."

"That's my thinking. I can't say for certain she knew Wilber, but there must be a reason she's here."

"Curt and Curtis overheard her … ."

"It might have been a setup. Otherwise, why would she willingly leave with them? I love Curt and Curtis, but they hardly look like men you'd want to go off in a truck with. I just want to make sure my friends are safe and that there's not another reason Gia is here," I said.

"You think she has a motive for being here?"

"We have to think about Wilber being murdered recently and possibly another person."

"What if Wilber murdered someone and buried the body on his property," Eleanor suggested.

"He was shot in his bed. It wasn't suicide."

"Revenge is a motivator. Someone might have found out that Wilber murdered someone."

"I don't believe that scenario, but I think I have an idea of who might have been murdered at Wilber's: Faith Fleur."

"The woman we thought was staying here."

"Exactly. I wonder why Jimmy led us to believe she was staying here."

"What about the black SUV?"

"It looks like we need to speak to Jimmy to sort this out."

Rosa Lee walked over with a smile. "What did you find out?"

"We were wrong. Her name isn't Faith Fleur," I said.

"That's a relief."

"Is it?" Eleanor asked. "You're boarding a complete stranger."

"She's all right. A little lost, but she'll get on track."

"Did Curt and Curtis tell you they were bringing home that girl before they showed up with her?"

"They called me first. I didn't care for the way it happened, but besides being a distraction for my boys she's no trouble at all. I can't say that for many of my boarders."

"You have a soft heart, but I caution you to watch your back. I don't believe Gia is who she's leading you to believe she is."

CHAPTER 8

Jimmy wasn't at the office or in the fenced-in impound yard. The receptionist said he was home. Jimmy's house was way out in the boonies. Sparsely spaced houses and trailers went by in a hurry as I floored it. It was hilly in this area and the station wagon seemed to be having trouble on the uptake.

Jimmy's house was a mobile home that had seen better days, but I noticed a foundation had been poured lately. It's about time he thinks about building that sweet wife of his a decent house. There's nothing wrong with living in a mobile home, but Jimmy had built a good business and he also made money from the county to use part of his yard as an impound lot. I rather thought of that as a perk in our investigations, although Jimmy wasn't always as helpful as we hoped. He could only do so much for us when cars were held for police investigations.

Dogs barked when we clambered out of the car, but I didn't see any run toward us. Jimmy walked out of his pole barn and motioned us over.

"I can't believe you're skipping work today," I said.

"I have to get this truck fixed or I can't go anywhere. The Mrs. won't appreciate it if I take her car again today."

"I imagine not when she has young children and you're impossible to get ahold of most of the day."

"You sound just like her." Jimmy laughed as he wiped his greasy hands on a rag. "What brings you by?"

"I was wondering why you told us Faith Fleur is staying with the Hills?"

"I told you before, that's what Curt and Curtis told me."

"We were just there. The woman staying there is Gia Swanson."

"She has jet black hair," Eleanor said.

"That doesn't sound right. I met Faith and she has blond hair."

"Could you have misunderstood what the Hills told you?"

"I don't see how." Jimmy scratched his head with a wrench. "I might not have been paying attention. I had Faith on my mind, I suppose. She's a real pretty girl."

"Don't forget you're married," I scolded Jimmy.

"Believe me, the Mrs. won't let me forget." He laughed.

"Take a look at this photo," Eleanor said. She showed Jimmy a picture of Gia on her cell phone. "Is this Faith?"

"This girl is pretty too, but she's not Faith."

"How are we going to know for sure?" Eleanor asked nobody in particular.

"I'll give Curt a call and ask him," I finally said.

I called Curt and asked him about what he'd told Jimmy, nodding at his response ending the call. "Apparently you must have forgotten you met Faith at the K of C fish fry last week. You were there with the Hill brothers. She contacted them later about a room for rent too, but Gia was already staying there."

"That's right, I was there picking up food for the Mrs."

"Why do so many women want to rent rooms at the Hill place?" Eleanor asked.

"I know neither of you are that old." Jimmy laughed. "Don't you know Curt and Curtis have always had the girls chasing after them?"

"Curt could barely ask Sally Alton out the one time."

"I said the girls chase them, not the other way around."

"We really appreciate your help, Jimmy," I said. "I knew there must have been a mix up. You've never steered us wrong."

"Hey wait. Don't we have a few more questions about the black SUV?" Eleanor asked.

"That's right. Have you seen that black SUV in town since two weeks ago?"

"I noticed yesterday that a black SUV was parked at Neiman's Family Market."

"Thanks for the tip." Eleanor winked.

"Gia mentioned she's on vacation in the area. She's staying with the Hills, but she told us her car broke down in town -- a Toyota Camry."

"I believe she told us it was towed," Eleanor added.

"I didn't tow it, but I'll check tomorrow first thing if anyone else did. We'd hate for the girl to be stuck at the Hills longer than she wants to be."

I shook my head as I laughed. "You don't want the Mrs. to hear you say that."

"And you'd better not tell her. Really, please don't tell her."

"I see you poured a foundation. Are you building a house after all these years?"

"Yes. I promised the wife I'd do that years ago, and I'm finally going ahead with it."

"You're a good husband, Jimmy," I said.

Eleanor and I walked back to the car and left in a flurry of gravel and dust.

"You know what's funny about Jimmy? He isn't in charge of his castle, his Mrs. is," Eleanor said.

"I can't imagine he's in the house much. Too much of grease monkey for that. I'm glad to hear he's building a house finally. That trailer is in bad shape even though the wife keeps it tidy. It's much too small for a family of five."

My stomach was growling by the time we arrived at Neiman's. A black SUV was parked in the furthest corner of the parking lot. How could I have missed it? Could it have been parked there for the last two weeks without anyone noticing?

Eleanor led the way inside, and dragged me to the bakery, where we selected doughnuts and poured the complementary coffee in the paperboard cups.

"Be careful not to slop the coffee on the floor," I said because Eleanor did that every time we came here.

I walked to the back of the store and rang the bell at the meat counter, and asked to see the manager. I stared at the thick steaks, which looked even better on an empty stomach.

"Can I help you?" a man dressed in a white shirt and black tie asked. He wore a nametag that read "Darrell."

"We're looking for a black SUV. I noticed you have one in the parking lot. Do you know who it belongs to?" I asked.

"The vehicle belongs to us. We use it to deliver groceries. Why?"

"It was seen at a crime scene," I said.

"Wh-What?" Darrell asked.

"Who was making deliveries two weeks ago?"

"Faith Fleur."

I almost bit my tongue off. "We really need to speak with her."

"Me too. She hasn't been here in two weeks."

"Can you describe her?"

"She's about five foot, five. Blond hair and green eyes."

"That sounds like someone we're looking for. Do you happen to have her address or phone number?"

"Don't bother trying to call her; it goes straight to voicemail."

We left after Darrell handed us an address and phone number scrawled on a piece of paper.

"Faith must be renting a room on Newman Street," I said after glancing at the address.

※

I KNOCKED ON THE DOOR AND A CHEERFUL WOMAN ANSWERED the door.

"Hello there," I said.

She cocked a brow. "I already have a church I attend."

I laughed. "We're investigators and we're looking for a young woman named Faith Fleur."

"We were told she rents a room here," Eleanor added.

"I'm looking for her too. She stiffed me a month's rent and I can't even toss her stuff out unless I go through the courts."

"When was the last time you saw her?" Eleanor asked.

"About two weeks ago. She promised she'd pay me that Friday, but she never showed up."

"She left her belongings behind?" I asked.

"They're still in her room."

"Can we look at them?" Eleanor asked.

I grabbed Eleanor's arm and whispered, "We can't."

"It's really important," Eleanor said. "We believe she's involved in a crime and there might be stolen merchandise in her room."

"Who did you say you were again?"

"We're investigators," I said.

"We work closely with Sheriff Peterson," Eleanor quickly added.

The woman frowned, her fingers grasping the yellow floral dress she wore.

"I suppose it won't hurt. I probably won't see her again anyway."

She directed us up the stairs and to the first room on the right. The stale smell blasted me in the face. "We need to open a window."

Eleanor shrugged as she opened the closet and looked through the clothing. "What are we looking for?"

"Anything that might tie her to Wilber's house," I said as I opened drawers and riffled through them.

Boxes tumbled to the floor from the top of the closet. I shook my head at Eleanor and helped her pick them up. I glanced inside the boxes, but they only contained winter clothing. "Faith must have planned to stay longer."

I helped Eleanor replace the boxes and then checked the bedside table before collapsing on the bed. "So much for finding anything of use."

Eleanor plopped on the bed next to me and yelled, "Ouch!" She pulled up the blankets and pulled out an address book and handed it to me.

I flipped through the book, which contained addresses and gas and food receipts until I ran across Wilber's address circled in red. "This proves Faith was at Wilber's house."

"I can't believe I found anything useful. See, sitting on a bed works sometimes. I'm a little tired," Eleanor admitted.

"I think we should call Sheriff Peterson. He needs to see this."

"Why don't we just go to the sheriff's department?"

"Because we can't remove this address book and I'm afraid to hide it here now that I know what it means."

"And our paws are all over the book."

"I know, but this is worth having Peterson yell at us."

"What is this supposed to be?" Peterson asked.

"It's an address book, what does it look like?" Eleanor smirked.

Peterson's face reddened. "Agnes, what is this?"

"It's Faith Fleur's address book."

"Who?"

"Faith Fleur."

"We found out Faith delivered groceries for Neiman's in a black SUV that belongs to the market," Eleanor added. "A vehicle matching that description was seen at Wilber's house a few days a week."

Peterson frowned. "Are we getting to a point soon?"

I stepped closer to Peterson. "The manager at Neiman's told us Faith hasn't been seen for a few weeks. Faith Fleur was the person murdered at Wilber's house."

"And this is her address book?" Eleanor shook the book. "Wilber's name is the book ... his address circled in red."

"Where did you find the book?"

"Here. Faith was renting this room and her landlady told us we could come up here and take a look. She's a little upset that Faith stiffed her on the rent."

"She hasn't been here for two weeks," Eleanor added.

Peterson shook his head. "Where did you find the book?"

"Under the covers."

"Why are you bringing this to my attention when you took it upon yourselves to go through the address book? You both know better than to handle potential evidence."

"At the time I wasn't sure it was evidence."

"We haven't found another body at Wilber's," Peterson said.

"Not yet you haven't. I suggest searching his property," I offered.

"We did. There isn't a blood trail to follow. It ends in the living room."

"Someone must have bagged the body and removed it," Eleanor said. "I wonder why they didn't remove Wilber's body."

"I have a feeling that we should be looking into Faith's past," I said. "Taking another look at Wilber's property wouldn't hurt."

"It's already been searched and anything found here can't be used. I don't have a warrant to search the premises. And if Faith delivered groceries to Wilber she very well could be a suspect, not a victim."

"You already have DNA you could check against Faith's toothbrush or hairbrush. You'll find the items in the bathroom."

"I'm leaving and you two need to do the same. You can't go through the woman's belongings and her landlady can't give you permission. Until Faith is evicted, her personal items can't be moved or thrown away."

"I don't need any trouble here," the landlady said. "I just want my money."

"Put the address book back where you found it," Peterson said. "I'll walk you out."

I lifted the covers to put the address book back. While Peterson looked the other way, I slipped it into Eleanor's purse.

"The sheriff is right. We'd better leave, Eleanor."

"I have to use the bathroom first."

Sheriff Peterson gave me a hard look, as if he knew we were up to something. Eleanor surfaced from the bathroom and I handed her her purse.

❦

WE PARTED WAYS WITH PETERSON AND I STARTED THE ENGINE AND drove off. "That was a waste," Eleanor said. "We should have never had Peterson come out there. And now we don't even have the address book."

"It's in your purse." I smiled.

"And her toothbrush is in my pocket."

"We are a good team, although I doubt we can get the DNA from Wilber's house checked against the toothbrush."

"What if we asked your granddaughter's husband."

I frowned and shook my head. "We won't get anywhere that way. Unless we find Faith's body."

"Well, we won't find it in the address book."

"No, but we might be able to track her movements with it."

"And check her past appointments and contacts. We might be able to find where she's from, so start making calls,"

"I'm driving to Wilber's house so we can take a look around."

"It's still a crime scene."

"I doubt the crime scene tape is still up, Eleanor."

"And what will you do if it is?"

I shrugged. "Help it blow away with wind?"

Eleanor made the calls and sighed in frustration when she exhausted the list. "So much for that. All the names in this book are customers she delivered groceries to."

"We'll find something else to go on. We always do."

I gritted my teeth at the sight of the crime scene tape when I drove into Wilber's driveway. Eleanor and I tried to wad it up without entangling ourselves in it.

We wandered into the overgrown backyard and searched for a trashcan on the back porch, but of course there wasn't one there. The cops had most likely taken it.

"Now where are we going to put this?" I asked.

"Maybe there's a trashcan in the house on the second floor."

"Peterson boarded the house up tight."

"We could check in the shed over there," Eleanor pointed out.

We walked to the shed that had a lean-to. It was locked. "We won't be able to get in," I said.

My eyes widened as Eleanor pulled on the door of the shed and tried to pry it open. I shook my head as I looked through the junk under the lean-to. "Can you help me?" I asked as I pulled out pieces of lumber.

"That's too big of a job for us."

"It's only a few boards. And look, there's a tarp and a roll of plastic."

Eleanor plugged her nose. "Yuck I'm not touching that smelly tarp!"

"Quit whining. You've picked up nastier things and brought them home." I grinned.

"Not funny, Mrs. Perfect."

My shoulders slumped. "I'm nowhere near perfect. My comment was out of line, sorry."

"Who are you and what have you done to my friend Agnes Barton? She doesn't apologize for her jokes."

"Don't you want to know what's under that tarp?"

"Spiders and creepy crawly bugs don't interest me."

"What if a body was wrapped inside it? Peterson mentioned there wasn't a blood trail, remember?"

"Fine, I'll help you clear this junk out. But we'll need to find a way inside the house so I can wash my hands."

Eleanor and I huffed and puffed and removed boards and a roll of plastic until we were finally able to reach the tarp. Sweat dripped down my face as we worked for the next ten minutes to remove the tarp.

"It's stuck," I said.

"It's too heavy to move by ourselves."

"It's probably full of rainwater."

Eleanor's eyes widened. "Among other things."

"I don't smell anything."

"What if it's wrapped in plastic?"

"It would still smell like rotting meat, I think."

"Then why are we moving the tarp?"

"To see if there is anything behind it," I said.

"Well, we can't budge it. We need help."

"It's too bad Jimmy was busy today. He's perfect in a pinch."

"I'll call him," Eleanor said. "The worst he can do say is no."

There was something behind the tarp that I couldn't quite see.

"He's not answering," Eleanor said as she held the phone against her cheek.

"Never mind. I'll call Andrew."

"Do you actually think he'll come out here and help us?"

"We won't know unless I call and ask."

I called Andrew, who promised to be right over.

"I wish there was somewhere we could sit," Eleanor said.

"How about the back porch?" I suggested.

Eleanor and I sat down on the porch and I wiped the remaining sweat from my brow.

"Wilber has a nice-sized backyard," Eleanor said. "I wonder if he has a burn barrel."

"A burn what?"

"You know, a big metal barrel you burn stuff in, branches and sticks that fall on the ground."

I twitched my nose. "I don't smell smoke."

"They probably didn't burn Faith's body here," Eleanor said.

"One of the neighbors would have called the fire department."

"Not for a burn barrel. Those aren't big enough to burn a body in."

"Unless the victim was small."

"Or in pieces."

I pressed a hand against my stomach. "Let's not go there."

I heard a car pull into the driveway and my heart hammered in my chest until Andrew rounded the corner.

"It's about time," I said.

"I'm going against my better judgment, but I'd rather be here in case something happens."

"What could happen?"

"I don't want to think about it."

Eleanor and I led Andrew to the lean-to, and between us three we pulled the tarp free. Andrew pulled up one side and water rushed out, along with spiders and bugs, as Eleanor had mentioned.

"There's a barrel back there," I pointed out.

"I'll roll it out," Andrew said.

Eleanor and I moved out of the way as Andrew strained to tip it over and roll it toward us. Once it was out of the lean-to, Andrew left us to retrieve tools from his car. He came back with a pry bar.

"We should set the barrel back up. It might be easier to remove the cover that way," I suggested.

Eleanor and I strained every muscle in our body and groaned as we helped Andrew right the barrel. He pulled and yanked on the tool until the seal of the barrel popped free. We fell to the ground at the stench that flooded the air and pressed our hands and shirts against our nostrils.

"I sure hope that's not what I think it is," I said.

CHAPTER 9

Andrew was the only one brave enough to glance inside the barrel. He escorted us to the back porch and called 911 with the discovery.

"I can't imagine someone stuffing a body in that barrel," Andrew said.

"I can't believe someone didn't get rid of the body," I said. "Seems to me that if you murdered someone you'd move the body to a different location."

"Sheriff Peterson didn't find the body and he searched the property," Eleanor said. "For some reason I expected to find a freshly-dug grave."

"Do you think Wilber might have murdered someone?" I asked.

"Wilber was too nice for that," Eleanor said.

"So people keep saying, but just because he's nice doesn't mean he didn't murder someone. Look how he treated Bernice when they divorced."

"But he didn't murder her."

"But he took her children."

"Who killed Wilber? Do you think it was common knowledge he was a murderer and was taken out by a vigilante?" Eleanor asked.

"If it was common knowledge someone would have turned him into the cops," Andrew said.

"Unless the person he murdered is related to the vigilante," I said.

"That's too far-fetched, and I'm sure Peterson will tell you the same," Andrew huffed.

"The crime happened inside, not outside," I told him.

"I doubt Peterson will think about it that way."

We met Peterson out front and he hiked up his pants as he approached.

"Why are you on an active crime scene, ladies?" His eyes then moved to Andrew. "Surprised to see you here, Hart."

"I am too, but believe me, I didn't think Agnes and Eleanor would really find anything out here."

"We called him to help us move a tarp," I said. "That's when we spotted the barrel."

"I can smell that you opened it before I even got here," Peterson said. "The state police crime lab boys will be here soon."

"I wonder if the blood on the carpet will match the remains," I said.

"I'd be shocked if it was the same person. Why put one body in the barrel and hide it here under our noses when Wilber's body was left out in the open?" Eleanor's lit up and she asked, "What if Wilber was a murderer?"

"Hard to have a victim you just killed kill you," Peterson countered. He frowned. "It looks like you might be right about one thing: We didn't search the property as well as we could have."

"I imagine you'd look for the same thing we thought of -- a recently-dug hole in the yard -- although with the grass this long it would be hard to see."

Peterson glanced across the unkempt lawn. "We should have the grass cut so we can take a closer look. What is really going on here?"

"Faith might be in the barrel," I suggested.

"I don't know if the remains are male or female. Believe me, I didn't need to take that good of a look inside." Andrew frowned. "Who is Faith?"

I quickly gave Andrew the rundown and he sighed. "So you believe Faith was the victim?"

"I don't know, but she hasn't been seen by anyone for a few weeks."

"We shouldn't jump to conclusions," Peterson said. "It could be anyone in that barrel."

"Are there any current missing persons reports?"

"None that I'm aware of. The victim might not even have ties to the area."

"So a missing person from another area?" Andrew asked.

"Or lured to the area," I added.

Peterson pulled a handkerchief from his pocket and swiped his face. "Someone else must be involved. I hope the body hasn't been in here too long. It will be harder to identify if there's been too much decomposition."

The sound of more cars pulling up stopped the conversation. Trooper Sales led the forensics team to join them. His brow furrowed as Bill locked eyes with me, but he remained silent as Sheriff Peterson led them to the barrel. "Go on home, Agnes. I'll speak with you later," Peterson said.

Andrew followed us to our car and we left separately. I wasn't certain who was more shocked about today's developments, Andrew or us. He was a corporate attorney and the job didn't involve finding dead bodies.

I adjusted the rearview mirror. "To be honest, I need to get the body and smell off my mind."

"Speaking of which, we both stink," Eleanor said. "We should freshen up before we go anywhere."

I dropped Eleanor off and went home to take a shower. Andrew wasn't home yet, which was fine by me. Duchess yawned when I brushed past the couch. She jumped down and padded to her litter box. I hurriedly scooped up the blanket with the kittens on it and placed it on a pet cushion on the floor. Ever since Duchess gave birth I was afraid that the kittens would kill themselves falling off the couch.

I hurried into the shower and dressed in cotton slacks and an aqua peasant shirt afterward. I changed into my much looser tennis shoes because my feet had swollen throughout the course of the day. I wore the sandal straps indentations on my skin like a badge and should have known it was important to have suitable footwear with an ongoing investigation.

I leisurely watered my houseplants that had sprung to life now that Duchess was too preoccupied with her offspring to rip them to shreds.

After that, I drove to Eleanor's house, where I found my partner engaged in a conversation with Elsie and Marjory.

"It's about time you got here, Agnes," Elsie said. "I thought you might want to hear the news from me first."

Eleanor's brow shot up and she sighed, which sounded much closer to a groan.

I gave my full attention to Elsie's pale face. "Bernice has flown the coop," Elsie gasped.

Silence was deafening as each of us were in shock at this revelation.

Eleanor elbowed her way between Marjory and Elsie, who thus far had remained silent. "I already told the girls that Bernice had assured us she'd stay in the hospital until Dr. Thomas released her," Eleanor said. "Isn't that right, Agnes?"

"That's what I thought she said, but this is Bernice we're talking about. You can't expect a cat lady to stay away from her felines for long," I said.

"Don't let Bernice hear you call her that," Elsie said.

"I call her Bernice," I said defensively. "All I was doing was ... oh never mind, we have more important matters at hand."

"How can you say that? Bernice is our friend," Marjory said with a shake of her head.

"That's what I meant." I shot Eleanor a look. "Didn't you tell them yet?"

"Tell us what?" Elsie asked.

"I thought I'd leave it up to you, Agnes," Eleanor said.

"I really wouldn't have minded, dear. I know you can't hold your tongue."

Eleanor crossed her arms defiantly. "It appears you're wrong ... again."

Marjory threw her arms heavenward. "Would someone tell us what's happened."

"Eleanor and I found remains on Wilber's property."

"I think we should sit on the deck. I'm feeling rather faint," Elsie said.

We congregated on the deck, and when everyone took a seat I asked, "Are you okay, Elsie."

Elsie fanned her face with a newspaper. "Of course. Do go on with what you were about to say."

"We found remains in a barrel on Wilber's property."

"Hidden in his backyard," Eleanor added, "next to his shed."

"However did you find it there?" Marjory asked.

"Well, it wasn't easy, and we had to call for reinforcements," I said.

"Andrew came over to help us," Eleanor added.

Elsie roared in laughter. "You mean he actually helped you? I can't believe it."

I gripped the arms of my lawn chair. "And why wouldn't he?"

"Because he's a little on the stuffy side," Elsie said.

"Look who's talking," I countered.

"Now girls this is no time to act like this," Marjory said. "What happened to poor Bernice should have taught all of us how fragile life really is."

"Shouldn't we be heading over to check on Bernice?" I asked.

"I don't know if Bernice needs to hear about what you found at Wilber's house while she's recovering."

"There's no keeping it from her for long. I expect the sheriff to question Bernice."

"He can't do that in her condition," Elsie gasped. "We'd better get over to Bernice's house before someone has the poor dear falling out."

"Only if you're feeling better, dear," I said.

⁂

I HOPPED OUT OF THE CAR AT BERNICE'S HOUSE WITH ELEANOR, Elsie and Marjory following me across the closely-cropped weeds that had overtaken her front yard. I hurried to her front door and barged inside.

Bernice lounged on the couch with a startled Callie at her side.

"What a surprise," Bernice announced.

"Elsie said something about you flying the coop and I had to find out if this was the coop she was referring to," I said.

Bernice slightly narrowed her eyes, but otherwise remained silent.

"I can't believe you told Elsie instead of us you were leaving the hospital," Eleanor complained.

"I knew if I told you, Agnes, that you'd interfere with my flight." She cackled. "You should have known that I can't stay away from my cats."

"Where are they? I didn't notice them when we drove up."

The color left Callie's face. "Well, th-that's b-be —."

"Spit it out, Callie," Bernice ordered.

"Angelo thought it might be a good idea if your cats were elsewhere when you returned."

"What did he do with them?" Eleanor asked.

"I-I'm not sure."

"You'd better call that brother of yours and get those cats back here," Eleanor shouted.

Bernice battered Callie back as she struggled to stand. "I can't believe Angelo has the muscle to take my cats anywhere."

"I have a hard time believing he wasn't mortally wounded trying." I said.

Callie made a call, which ended with her shrugging. "It went straight to voicemail."

"Should we take Bernice to the pound?" Elsie asked.

"We should check to see if Angelo is in the emergency room," I said. "It would teach him to take one of Bernice's beloved felines."

Bernice walked through the house and out the back door. Eleanor and I hurried after her.

Bernice's hands slipped to her hips. "My cats are over there." She smiled as she sat on a lawn chair. "His evil plans have been thwarted. Taking my cats would be the only motive for murder if I ever killed anybody."

"I wish you wouldn't say that," I said.

"Especially after the find on Wilber's property," Eleanor said.

Bernice cocked a brow.

"Bernice isn't healthy enough to get stressed again," Elsie said.

Bernice rolled her eyes. "What finding is this?"

I explained to Bernice about what Eleanor and I found at Wilber's house.

Bernice's lower lip protruded. "What does the sheriff have to say about it?"

"He's just like us, confused," I said. "There were bloodstains on Wilber's living room carpet that didn't belong to him."

"Agnes, that's too much information for Bernice," Marjory cautioned.

"I'm hardly a fragile flower," Bernice protested. "What do you make of it, Agnes and Eleanor?"

"How well do you know Wilber, I mean really? Since you reconnected with him, has he done anything that set the alarms off inside your head?" I asked.

"The only alarms that man set off are in my heart," Bernice admitted. "I know you think I'm a hardened woman and it must be strange hearing me talk like this about my ex-husband, but despite our past that man was the love of my life."

"Oh, Mother," Callie called out as she hugged Bernice.

Bernice stiffened and pushed her daughter away. "It's not that easy, daughter. You can't expect me to forgive you so easily after the way you and your brother treated me just the other day. I didn't see either of you at the hospital."

"That was because we were arrested," Callie said as she staggered back.

"They were held for questioning," Eleanor clarified. "Did you give your mother a ride from the hospital, Callie?"

"Sophia brought me home," Bernice said.

"I didn't see her car in the driveway," I said.

"Bill dropped her off after he received a call to report to work."

"Probably to the crime scene at Wilber's house."

"Sophia is upstairs cleaning. Bill dropped the baby off at Martha's."

"That's a relief. This place is too dangerous for a baby."

"You might be right. There is nothing baby-proofed in this house." Bernice forced a smile. "I had hoped to have grandchildren of my own someday, but my children don't want anything to do with me."

"I'm here now," Callie protested.

"Guilty conscience."

Callie walked back inside, and I asked, "Are you sure you haven't misjudged Callie?"

"You weren't here that day."

"We were after the fact," Eleanor said.

"And Callie seemed very concerned about you," I said.

"Don't let her fool you like she's fooled me. One minute my children were fine with me and the next they wanted nothing to do with me. They only came over that day to accuse me of murdering their father."

"They overreacted," Elsie said. "But we all make mistakes. Give Callie another chance."

"I don't know if I have enough time left for second chances."

"There's always time for second chances," I said. "I'm living proof of that when my daughter Martha showed up. Sophia can tell you all about how she didn't want anything to do with Martha when she came to town."

"Grams is right," Sophia said as she walked outside and took a load off. Her dark hair was held back with a handkerchief. "My mother left town without telling me where she went after my parents divorced."

Martha had been off the grid and none of the family had been able to contact her. I felt just as bad about Martha's absence. I felt as though I had done something wrong. I had been kept in the dark about Martha's disastrous marriage, but my daughter allowed me to pick up Sophia for the summers. In many ways I lived for those summers.

"Who cut your lawn?" I asked.

"Lawn?" Elsie laughed.

"Bill had the weeds bushwhacked," Sophia said. "He said it's not safe for Bernice to be walking around the yard in thigh-high weeds."

"Weeds? They're like trees," Eleanor said.

"Do you think Wilber was capable of killing anyone, Bernice?" I asked.

Bernice's eyes met mine. "Do you think Wilber killed that woman?"

"I didn't say anything about the remains being male or female."

"It had to be female with Wilber's background," Bernice said with tears in her eyes.

"I can't believe you. My father was not a murderer," Callie shouted as she stomped outside. "Even if he happened to have been in relationships with a crazed woman at one time." Her face lit up. "Maybe she was the one who killed those women."

"Those women?" Eleanor asked.

"I think you need to explain yourself," I said.

"My dad was questioned in the past for the disappearances of female hitchhikers when Angelo and I were younger."

"Was he a truck driver?"

"Salesman," Bernice said. "Wilber wasn't living in Tawas back then."

"That doesn't make him less a murderer," I said.

Callie came running at me. "My father didn't —."

Bernice quickly separated us. "Wilber didn't own that property back then, isn't that right, Callie?"

"That's what I was trying to say."

"You go at my grandmother like that again and I'll box your ears," Sophia said as she menacingly walked toward Callie.

"Try it and I'll call the cops," Callie said.

"I'm married to the cops," Sophia retorted.

"Settle down, ladies," Marjory said. "Not that I'm not enjoying the friendly exchange. I had no idea you knew how to box, Sophia."

"Bill taught me."

"Why would you even mention your father's possible involvement with missing female hitchhikers?" I asked. "Do you think it was a woman's body found on your father's property?"

"So it was a woman?" Callie asked.

"We don't know who it was for certain," Eleanor said. "And we might not for some time. We really came here to see how Bernice was faring."

"I think I should leave. All I'm doing is causing problems," Callie said.

"You can't run away now, not unless you want your mother to think you're not worthy of a second chance. She needs you now."

"Keep that brother of yours away from here," Sophia said. "Your mother needs to rest."

"She's right. Eleanor and I didn't mean to upset you, but we had to ask you about Wilber."

"I imagine the sheriff will be back here soon asking questions. If there was a bloodstain on Wilber's carpet, you can't be suggesting that he murdered someone and hid the body on his property. He was murdered in his sleep," Bernice said.

"We haven't worked it all out, but I can't help wondering if someone might have caught wind of the murders Wilber was accused of and caught up to him."

"Why would they hide the other body if they killed my father?" Callie asked.

"That's a good question," I said.

"My father was a smart man. He'd get rid of the body if he killed anyone."

"Are you talking from personal experience?" Eleanor asked.

Callie met Bernice's eyes briefly before focusing back on Eleanor and me. "I would think you'd be more concerned with finding out who murdered my father, not worrying about some body that might have been found on the property."

"It was definitely found on your father's property," I said. "If your father was a person of interest in missing person cases in the past, it might have come back to haunt him."

"Someone might have gone to prison for the crimes and recently was released," Eleanor added.

"I hope we haven't upset you further, Bernice. We really are concerned about you," I said.

"Bernice, I think under the circumstances you should come and stay with me and Jack until the killer is found," Elsie said.

Bernice's eyes widened. "You and Jack? I can't imagine he'd want me over at your place."

"We're staying at my house and I have a spare bedroom."

"We'll bring you over every day to check on your cats," Marjory said.

Bernice thumped her fingers on her stomach. "That sounds like a right good idea."

"Mother, I told you I'd stay with you until you felt better," Callie said.

"Under the circumstances I'd feel safer at Elsie's house."

Callie's face fell. "I'd never do anything to harm you, Mother."

"No, you and your brother just want me in jail for killing your father. You've both said as much the other day when I had my episode. I'd never kill Wilber. He was the only man I've ever loved."

Callie's eyes narrowed. "If you really loved him you would never have driven him away."

"And I suppose it's your mother's fault your father was a no good cheat?" Eleanor asked. "I would think after all these years that you'd open your eyes to the truth. Your father prevented you from knowing your own mother while you were growing up."

CHAPTER 10

I pulled next to Sheriff Peterson's cruiser at Nieman's, and Eleanor and I waited by his car until he returned, carrying two plastic store bags.

His brow furrowed as he asked, "What are you doing here?"

"Did you ask the manager about Faith Fleur?" I asked.

"Yes, and he confirmed what you told me. I'll have you know nobody has filed a missing person report yet. And then I did a little shopping."

"I have some interesting information to share."

Peterson put his purchases in the squad car and then gave me his full attention. "If you can be brief. I have ice cream."

Eleanor cocked a brow. "Aren't you on a diet?"

"It's for a birthday party."

"Whose birthday?" I asked. "Are we invited?"

"No. Neither of you are." Peterson put a hand on his open door. "I really need to get going."

"Fine. We paid Bernice a visit. She went AWOL from the hospital."

"Agnes, tell the sheriff what we came here for," Eleanor prodded.

"Callie was at Bernice's house. She let it slip that her father was a suspect in a string of missing female hitchhikers when she and her brother were children."

Peterson's eyes widened. "Did she mention how long ago?"

"I'd imagine the late nineties."

"Not too many women hitchhikers in the nineties."

"That's what I thought," Eleanor said. "Is there any way you can check for cold cases?"

"Sounds like a crapshoot, but I'll relay this to the state police. They might have more resources to search cases you're referring to."

"And you don't have the time to do it yourself?" I asked.

"I'm busy enough handling the active cases in this county. What are you hinting at?"

"Well, we just thought that if Wilber was involved in those disappearances someone from his past might have tracked him down."

"And whacked him," Eleanor added, drawing a finger across her throat.

"A victim's family member?" Peterson asked.

"Or someone might have wrongfully gone to prison for the crime and was just released," I added.

Peterson crossed his arms. "Then we would be talking about cold cases, which are even more of a needle in the haystack."

"Did the coroner give you a preliminary report yet?"

"I don't even know if forensics removed the body from the barrel yet. They have custody of it now."

"So how long will it take to find out if the victim is male or female?"

"You'll have to ask the coroner."

"Are you encouraging us to question the coroner?" Eleanor asked.

"Not at all, but you two seem hell bent on doing whatever you want."

"Do you have any other suspects right now?" I asked.

"I'm coming up empty at the moment. Have you interviewed Wilber's neighbors yet?"

"We questioned Robert Boyd, but the only useful information he offered was that a black SUV was parked at Wilber's house." I pointed out the SUV parked in the corner of the parking lot. "That one over there, I believe. Did you obtain a search warrant for Faith's room or the SUV yet?"

"She's not missing unless someone files a report."

"I'll bet the manager of Neiman's would allow you to take a look in the SUV."

Peterson looked into his car. "I suppose I could do that, but it will have to wait until tomorrow," he said as he sat in his cruiser. "Let me know if you find out about those missing hitchhikers. I know you have your resources."

I watched as Peterson peeled out from the parking lot and roared up the road.

"What did he mean 'resources?'" Eleanor asked.

I frowned for a moment until the bell rang in my head. "He's right. I do have my own resource, and I'll contact him later. But first we're going to take a look at the SUV."

"You think the manager will let us?"

"It's either that or we'll find our own way inside."

※

"Has anyone driven the black SUV parked outside since Faith went missing?" I asked Darrell, the manager.

I swear I could see the perspiration marks under the arms of his shirt growing. "No, it's been sitting there ever since. It won't start, and I haven't made the time to have a mechanic take a look."

"Would you mind if we took a look? There might be a clue inside that will help us find Faith."

"So you didn't find Faith at the address I gave you?"

"Nope. And the sheriff can't get a search warrant to search her room because nobody has filed a missing person report."

"She hasn't been seen by her landlady for a few weeks either," Eleanor said.

"I'll be right back," Darrell said as he disappeared into the backroom.

I admired the steaks and inhaled the fragrance of the raw meat as a vampire would. I'd sure love to bring home a few steaks.

Darrell returned and handed me the keys. "Let me know what you find. I've been worried about Faith since I talked to you two the last time."

"Were you close to her?" Eleanor asked.

"She was a good employee. The customers liked her."

"So, nothing personal?" I asked.

Darrell cleared his throat. "I considered Faith a model employee and friend. Nothing more. She's given me good advice in the past. I forgot my anniversary last year and she made a few suggestions for this year." He smiled thoughtfully. "And now my wife is pregnant."

"That's some suggestion," Eleanor said with a wolfish grin.

"Congratulations," I said as I took the keys and walked back outside.

"I can't believe Darrell gave us the keys," Eleanor said. "We should have asked for plastic gloves in case we find anything important."

"Leave it to me." I fished in my purse and waved latex gloves. "I have it covered."

I unlocked the vehicle with the key fob after we gloved up. "Well, the battery isn't dead. I wonder if the engine still runs."

I jumped into the driver's seat and stepped on the brake and pressed the button of the keyless ignition. The engine roared to life. I quickly turned it off. "It appears someone had the SUV fixed," Eleanor said with a frown.

"What are you suggesting?"

"That Faith and Darrell were closer than he suggested. There must be some reason nobody else has driven this vehicle."

"We'll ask him that after we search for evidence."

"Which won't be worth anything without a search warrant."

"I'll bet Darrell would let Peterson take a look too," I insisted. "If we find anything, that is."

I opened the armrest and waded through a boatload of paper; registration and proof of insurance. I ran across a wad of dollar bills, loose change, pens and a receipt book. I glanced at the pages of the receipt book closely. I took a glove off and rubbed my finger gently on a page. I could feel indentations.

"I know you're not going to take that, Agnes."

"I think we can see at least the last page if we handle it right."

"Which will be useless if it's a vital clue."

"It will further our investigation."

"And set back the police investigation."

"Since when are you such a worrywart?"

"When you began planning to destroy evidence. If Faith was the one in the barrel, the killer might never see a prison cell. I don't want to be responsible for that."

I sighed. "You're right of course," I said as I put it back. "We'd better hope we find something else."

Eleanor handed me two receipts, one from Day's Inn and the other from Bambi's Motel. I snapped a photo with my iPhone and set them on the seat.

I checked under the seats, finding only empty candy and gum wrappers.

"I found a McDonald's bag under my seat," Eleanor announced and opened it with a grin. She then frowned, her plus-sized body trembling. "I think you might want to take a look."

I took the bag and glanced inside. It was filled with cash. "Peterson might not want to be bothered," I said. "But we'll have to give him a call."

Eleanor made the call and we walked back inside to speak with Darrell, who strangely enough seemed to be waiting for us behind the meat counter. He held a clipboard and pen. So he was writing down the temperatures of the cases of meat and not waiting after all.

Eleanor began, "We found something interesting in the... ."

"Is there a reason the SUV started when you told us it wasn't operational?" I interjected.

"What was really going on between you and Faith?" Eleanor asked with narrowed eyes. "There must be some reason nobody has used the vehicle to deliver groceries in the past two weeks."

"Especially when Faith quit coming to work," I added.

Darrell sighed. "It's not what you think. I expected Faith back next week. She told me she would be in Oscoda taking care of a sick aunt."

"Why didn't you tell us that?"

"Because I promised not to."

"What's the name of this sick aunt?" I asked, "unless you plan on having the sheriff charge you with obstruction of justice. She might be a suspect in Wilber's murder."

Darrell's mouth slacked open. "I'll be right back."

"And we'll go with you just in case you plan to slip out the back," Eleanor said.

"Good idea," I said as I followed Darrell and Eleanor into the meat cutting room. The room was empty; the butchers only worked until two.

Darrell walked into his cluttered office and came back with a notebook and jotted down an address.

"You seem to be jotting that down from memory," I said.

"I've met Faith's aunt before."

"Well, isn't that cozy," Eleanor said as she rolled back on her heels and then winced. So much for acting like a super sleuth. I'd sprain my ankle if I tried a number like that.

"She shops here!" Darrell protested.

"There's a grocery store in Oscoda. Perhaps Faith brought her aunt here so she could schmooze with you."

"There's no place like Nieman's Family Market."

"He's right about that," Eleanor said. "How are deliveries paid for?"

"By credit or debit card."

"So no cash purchases?" I asked.

"If there is any cash in that vehicle it would be Faith's tips."

"She has some big tippers," Eleanor exclaimed, grinning until I shot her a look.

"I'm hoping you'll let Sheriff Peterson take a look at the vehicle," I said. "He should be here momentarily."

"We found something in the SUV that he'll be interested in. Are you sure Faith didn't carry cash with her on deliveries?" Eleanor asked.

"I'm positive. It's not safe. I even have a small sign on the back stating that."

Sheriff Peterson was waiting for us by the meat counter when we resurfaced from the back room. His face was drawn, bags beneath his eyes. "Are you giving me permission to search the SUV Faith Fleur has been using?" he asked.

"Yes, of course. Anything that will help find her."

It was interesting that Darrell didn't mention that Faith was supposedly at her aunt's house in Oscoda. It didn't bother me because it's the first place Eleanor and I would be going after we left Neiman's.

We walked with the sheriff outside and he unlocked the SUV. "So what's so interesting in the SUV?"

I rattled off the notable items, excluding the cash.

"I found a McDonald's bag full of cash," Eleanor said. "A lot of it."

Peterson gloved up and began checking the seats as Trooper Sales pulled up. Together they searched the vehicle. "We'll handle it from here," Peterson said. "Where did you say you found that bag full of cash?"

"Under the seat," I said.

"You might want to take a look at a receipt book," I said.

"If you two were younger I'd tell you to go to the academy," Trooper Sales said.

"They'd never make good cops; they don't know how to follow orders," Peterson retorted.

"The manager said there shouldn't be any cash in the vehicle."

"The deliveries are paid by credit or debit cards," Eleanor added.

"Thanks ladies," Peterson said. "You can run along now."

Run along, I grumbled in my head as Eleanor and I climbed in our car and I skidded back on 23 heading to Oscoda.

CHAPTER 11

I pulled up to a large beach house in Oscoda. "Are you sure this is the right address, Eleanor?"

"That's the address Darrell wrote down."

"This place is huge. Must cost a pretty penny," I said as we walked up to the double-paned glass doors.

A woman answered, her cheeks flushed, sweat pooling between her breasts in the sports bra. She also wore shorts and athletic shoes.

"I hope we're not interrupting your workout, Ms. Brighton," I said.

"You're Ellen Brighton aren't you," Eleanor said.

"Yes, and who are you?"

"We're here to talk to you about your niece, Faith Fleur," I said.

"I don't know anyone by that name."

"The manager at Neiman's told us Faith was here taking care of you. He assured us he met you."

Ellen began to close the door in our face. "We're investigators," I said. "It seems that someone has led us astray."

"Have you seen anyone who might fit Faith's description? She's five foot, five, with blond hair and green eyes."

The door opened more. "It sounds like the last house sitter, but her name was Bunny Vaverick. She didn't have green eyes, hers were shimmer blue."

"Shimmer blue?" Eleanor asked.

"They're fake contact lenses that the younger kids these days wear. They have glitter in them, I believe."

"You mean it looks like glitter," I said. "FDA-approved, I hope."

"I couldn't tell you."

"Getting back to Bunny, how long ago did you use her?"

"Up until a few days ago. I live in Auburn Hills and arrived a few days ago. Why?"

"We've been told she's been missing for about two weeks."

"She might have forgotten to tell anyone where she went," Ellen offered.

"That must be it."

"Did she mention a forwarding address?" Eleanor asked. "It's very important that we find her. Her family is worried about her."

Ellen cocked a brow. "Just a minute."

She gently closed the door and a few minutes later handed us an address. "I'm not sure if she's still here, but it's where I was told to send her final paycheck."

"That's quite official for a house sitter."

"It's an expense I use as a corporate deduction."

"I see. Have you noticed anything missing from your house?" Eleanor asked.

"No, why?"

"It's just that we believe your house sitter was in possession of a large amount of cash. We hope she didn't steal it from you."

Ellen smiled. "Not unless she's a safe cracker."

"And when was the last time you opened the safe?"

"You know I don't believe I have. Come inside. My neighbors are beginning to get curious."

I popped a glance over my shoulder and sure enough neighbors stood in a group on the corner pretending not to notice us. Oscoda is a small town, so that didn't surprise me, although I certainly hoped they'd be there when we came out. Snoopy neighbors can be a good source of information.

Eleanor and I followed Ellen across the marble floor and were instructed to wait. My eyes bugged out as I admired the interior of the house. Vaulted ceilings with a skylight. A spiral staircase with a crystal chandelier hanging over the top of the stairs. I admired my reflection in the banister that smelled of lemon oil.

"I'm not missing anything," Ellen announced as she rejoined us. "I feel better knowing that, but there's no way anyone could access this door."

She demonstrated the four steel bars that came out of the door when the lock was turned.

"Now that's great security," Eleanor admired.

"It's a panic room."

"I've heard of those, but I've never seen one."

"Let's go, Eleanor. We appreciate your help, Ellen."

"You're welcome, and I'm sorry I almost slammed the door in your face."

We walked back to the car and I made a detour in the direction of Ellen's neighbors, who were still congregated on the corner.

"Hello, ladies," I greeted them. "I was wondering if you could help us."

"We're investigators and we were curious about your neighbor over there." Eleanor pointed to the house we'd just left.

"Ellen Brighton," I said.

"Oh, I hope Ellen hasn't done anything wrong," the taller of the gray-haired ladies said.

"Oh no, nothing like that. We were led to believe that she arrived in town only a few days ago."

"That sounds about right."

"And she had a house sitter here while she was gone?" Eleanor asked.

"Yes, a rather friendly young lady. Spent the majority of her time sunning herself."

"I don't think she did much cooking," a shorter woman said. "Her fast-food wrappers blew across the street." She clucked her tongue. "I hate to pick up after someone, but I don't want the neighborhood trashed. I'd hate for our property values to go down."

I couldn't blame them for wanting to keep their neighborhood trash free. Oscoda has a lovely stretch of beach and an amazing view of Lake Huron.

"Did you happen to catch the woman's name?" Eleanor asked.

"We only waved at her," the tall woman said and her gaggle of friends nodded profusely.

"Does Ellen frequently have someone watching her house while she's down state?"

"Ellen had a break-in a few years ago. She's become an alarmist."

"I would think it would concern all of you," Eleanor said.

"Not to the point of having an elaborate security system, but I assume Ellen is quite wealthy. Her beach house is the most expensive in Oscoda."

"Is there anything else you could add about Ellen's house sitter?" I asked. "What kind of car did she drive?"

"One of those SUVs that are popular these days."

"A black one?" Eleanor asked.

"I believe it was white."

"It had a Kohler's Flowers sign on the side," the shorter woman said. "She delivers flowers for Kohler's."

"Thank you ladies," I said.

Eleanor chuckled as we drove to the address Ellen gave us. "Leave it to the neighbors to tell us the house sitter spent the majority of her time sunning herself."

"I wonder how they'd know. I imagine Ellen has a private beach and a brick wall conceals her patio and lake view."

"Binoculars."

"I'm glad my neighbors aren't that close," I said.

"Most of my mine are weekenders," Eleanor said. "My map app says we should turn on the next street."

I made the turn and pulled up to a two-story house. A white SUV with the flower sign was parked in the driveway.

Eleanor knocked on the door and a young lady about my height with blond hair pulled up into a bun answered the door. Her contact lenses were definitely decorative. I was lost in the sparkles until Eleanor nudged me.

"Hello there," I began when the girl didn't greet me. "Are you Bunny Vaverick?"

"Who's asking?" the young lady asked in a little girl-like voice. Her hand moved to a bony hip.

"We're investigators from Tawas. Ellen Brighton gave us your address."

"I hope Ellen isn't upset with me. I'd really like to work for her again."

"You were her house sitter, is that correct?"

"Ellen didn't have a bad word to say about you," Eleanor quickly said.

"Then why are you here?"

"We're investigating a crime in Tawas," I said. "Actually, we were surprised that you were housesitting for Ellen."

"We were told Faith Fleur would be there," Eleanor added.

Bunnie nodded. "I asked Faith to housesit for me, but she bowed out at the last minute."

"How long ago was that?" I asked.

"About two weeks ago. It's not like her to do that. She's quite dependable for someone our age." She grinned.

"Was Ellen aware that Faith would be housesitting instead of you?"

"Oh no, but I planned to introduce her to Ellen."

"It seems to me that might make Ellen feel a little uncomfortable. She seems like the type who would want to check out a sitter thoroughly."

Bunny frowned. "Believe me, she's exactly like that. But I had planned to go to Traverse City for a few days. Thanks to Faith, I couldn't go."

"I'm sure you'll have another opportunity."

"Not with my job. I'm kept busy."

"Is that your SUV?" I asked.

"It's a company vehicle. I deliver flowers for Kohler's Flowers. The owner allows me to take the SUV home."

"That's kind of her," Eleanor said. "Has Faith ever delivered flowers?"

"That's how I met her. She delivered flowers for my grandmother's birthday and we got to talking. She helped me get the job at Kohler's. Faith took a position delivering groceries for Neiman's Market."

"How good of friends are you?"

"We're not best friends or anything, but I've bumped into her at the Irish pub in town. It's a great little bar if you like a friendly atmosphere and killer drinks."

"I'll have to keep that in mind," Eleanor said. "Agnes and I like to toss one back every so often."

"Did Faith ever mention Darrell, the manager at Neiman's?" I asked.

"I already told you —."

"You weren't that good of friends with Faith, got it," Eleanor interjected.

"Why would you ask Faith to stand in for you as a house sitter if you weren't that close?"

"I was desperate."

"Let me a guess. You were hoping to get alone time with a certain man in Traverse?" Eleanor grinned.

"Yes, but it didn't work out for me. It turns out he wasn't that in to me. It's probably good I couldn't go to Traverse."

"Men."

"Thank you for your time, Bunny," I said. "One last question: Did Faith tell you she was Ellen's niece? She claimed she was taking care of her sick aunt."

"Sounds like she had to make up a story to get time off work."

My shoulders slumped when Eleanor and I walked back to the car. I drove back onto 23. I had hoped Bunny would have something more to say about Faith. Instead of getting another clue we'd hit a brick wall again.

"That was disappointing. I'd hoped that Bunny would be able to tell us more about Faith," I finally said.

"She didn't even seem to know Faith that well."

"We have a few questions. Why did Faith tell Darrell she was staying with a sick aunt two weeks ago?"

"You saw that beach house. It's gorgeous."

"Still, that's quite the story."

"It doesn't change the timeline," Eleanor said. "Faith hasn't been seen for two weeks."

"It might be time to touch base with the coroner."

"Even if he could tell us if the remains are male or female it will take time to identify the body and cause of death."

"Let's just hope the body didn't decompose as fast as Peterson believes."

Oscoda, a quaint town, also had a G's Pizzeria, although not as fancy as the one in Tawas. You could order a beer with your cheese pizza too. Right next to that was the Bavarian Bakery and Restaurant, and I had to make a quick stop. You can't get fresh bakery style doughnuts just anywhere, and I'd rather purchase local as opposed to chain coffee shops. Not that Eleanor and I don't love Tim Hortons. Nobody else makes a peanut crunch doughnut like that.

The buzzer over the door sounded and we made our way to the bakery display case, where we practically drooled on the glass.

A woman around our age approached the counter and waited for nearly ten minutes before we made our selections. I paid for our purchase and admired the menu board for the breakfast special. They served breakfast all day, but you couldn't get the special after eleven. I wished I had more time in the morning to come down here. I suppose I could if I really tried, but that never seemed to work out. If I dared do it without Eleanor alongside me I'd never hear the end of it. Honestly, it would be hard to have breakfast without my friend and partner.

Eleanor shoved the doughnut in her mouth and I pulled into a gas station and bought two diet pops. I shook my head at her chipmunk cheeks. "Seriously, Eleanor, you're going to choke to death one day. Do me a favor and don't do it when you're with me."

"You act like you don't enjoy wrapping your arms around me, Agnes."

I smiled knowing Eleanor was merely goading me for a hasty retort, but instead I simply put my chin up and drove to Kohler's Flowers.

Eleanor wiped off her mouth and fingers before we walked inside. My nose twitched at the assault of fragrances that trailed up my nostrils. I tried my best to breathe through my mouth. I've been known to have asthma attacks in florist shops.

Shelves were packed full of figurines for funerals. Angels had the largest shelf. No surprise there. Planter-type birdhouses with twig poles were scattered on the floor.

"Hello," I greeted the woman at the counter.

"How can I help you ladies today?" she asked.

"We're looking for information about Faith Fleur. We were told she works here."

"Worked here," Eleanor put in with a slight smile.

"Faith worked here about six months ago before she decided delivering groceries was her new dream job." The woman laughed.

"Didn't she suggest Bunny Vaverick would be a good fit for delivering?" I asked.

"Bunny works for me now, though she had to take two weeks off to housesit. I suppose the girl needed a vacation. I'm glad she'll be back tomorrow."

"Getting back to Faith," Eleanor said. "What was she like?"

"She has a talent for her job and was always willing to help out here at the shop. Some of the customers find Bunny's Barbie doll voice irritating." She smiled.

"So no problems with Faith?"

"Not in the least."

"Would you call her dependable?"

"Of course. Why are you asking me all these questions about Faith? Are you planning to hire her?"

"I wish that was the case. She's missing, I'm afraid."

"And we're trying to find her," Eleanor said.

"She hasn't been seen for two weeks, which has concerned us because everyone we've spoken with has given us the same story."

The woman pressed a hand against her chest. "How awful. I hope you find her. It breaks my heart to think that something untoward has happened to her."

"We're hoping she has forgotten to tell her family where she's gone."

"Young ladies seem to do that sort of thing at times," Eleanor said with a shake of her head.

"I'm afraid you're mistaken. Faith doesn't have any family. She's on her own and that can't be easy in this area. Not many high-paying jobs in town. Even us business owners have a hard time keeping it going."

"You have a lovely flower shop," I said.

"And I normally keep busy, but not always in the off season."

"I'll make sure to recommend your shop," I said. "You have quite a variety and I have a few friends who are obsessed with angel figurines."

"Why thank you."

CHAPTER 12

"Stop by Marion's Dairy Bar when we get back to Tawas."

"Won't it spoil our dinner?" I asked.

"We actually have time for dinner today? From the way you're pushing us I thought we couldn't sleep until we solved this case."

I looked over at Eleanor and saw how tired she was from the way her shoulders drooped.

"It sure seems that way, but we'll call it quits after some ice cream. I imagine Andrew and Mr. Wilson are wondering where we disappeared to."

"If you've ever noticed, they don't seem to be as put out as they once were. They know when we're on a case we get a little single-minded."

"Yes, like a dog searching for his bone," I agreed.

I pulled into the parking lot behind G's Pizzeria and we hoofed it to Marion's. The statue of a little boy holding an ice cream cone beckoned us closer and the fragrance of waffle cones wafted in the air. I could taste the creamy goodness already.

It wasn't too crowded inside and that was a blessing. Eleanor ordered a hot fudge sundae and I had a pineapple with the works. It wasn't a sundae without whipped cream and chopped nuts. I paid the cashier and Eleanor I looked for an open booth.

I stopped in shock when I spotted Curt and Curtis Hill with Rosa Lee's boarder Gia. She wore a crop top and shorts that showed plenty of skin. The boys didn't notice us as Curt was feeding Gia a spoonful of his ice cream sundae. Curtis glared on from narrowed eyes, his hands clenched into fists.

"Curt and Curtis, fancy meeting you here," I said hoping to defuse the situation.

"Why hello, Gia," Eleanor said. "I hope you don't mind if we sit with you."

Curtis scooted over so that Eleanor and I could sit next to him.

It was a tight squeeze and I tried not to elbow Curtis as I had my first spoonful of sundae. "This tastes heavenly."

"We've had a long day," Eleanor seconded. "So what have you boys been up to lately?"

"Showing Gia around town," Curtis said.

"She's looking for a job and we're helping her," Curt added.

"But I thought she was working at Dairy Queen."

"It didn't work out," Gia said with a shrug.

From the look of Gia's mussed hair I couldn't see her as high class and from New York City. You could be from there and not be high class and it wouldn't matter to me. I just hated the pretentiousness of her claim.

"Have you gotten any bites yet?" I asked.

Gia shook her head sadly. "Nothing that fits my skills."

"Oh, I didn't know you had any skills," Eleanor said as she popped a glance at Gia.

Gia blinked her eyelashes and popped her spoon in her mouth. "I was an administrative secretary in New York for a major law firm."

"What law firm is that?" I asked. "My husband is an attorney; he might know it."

"He's spent time in New York," Eleanor added.

Gia glanced down at her melting sundae. "Wilson and Gunter. They're divorce lawyers," she said when she glanced up.

I made a metal note to check to see if there really was a Wilson and Gunter practicing divorce law in New York.

"No wonder you came to Michigan," Eleanor said. "That sounds so depressing."

"Very. Especially when a husband or wife loses custody of children. It's very tragic for all parties involved."

"Did you quit that job?" Eleanor asked.

"I believe she said vacation the other day," I said.

"I'm on a personal leave, actually. I really needed a break."

"What are your plans if you don't find a job in town?" I asked.

Gia wiped spilled ice cream off the table. "I suppose I'll have to move on."

That's what I wanted. I didn't like the wedge that was between the Hill brothers. I suspected she was playing them both.

"You don't have to do that," Curt said. "Ma said you can stay as long as you need."

I clenched my hand into a fist. Did Rosa Lee really say that or was it her son's wishful thinking? It didn't sound like her at all, especially when she considered Gia a distraction around her place. Oh well, it's none of my business. It's just that Curt and Curtis deserved so much better. Not that I can say they're great catches. Neither of them has shown the slightest interest in a long-term relationship. I didn't consider them mama's boys, but they might not be the type of men who wanted to be tied down.

Eleanor and I finished our sundaes and bid the trio goodbye. "Tell your mother we said hi," I said as we left.

"Dinner will have to wait. I'm stuffed," Eleanor said.

"We'll have to give our husbands an excuse for why we can't have dinner yet. If we can even find them. I haven't heard from Andrew since we found the remains."

"I bet they're at my house," Eleanor offered.

I drove below the speed limit all the way to Eleanor's house. There were times when I just wanted a relaxing drive. It helped me think, and right now I knew what we had to do. I just hoped my son Stuart would be reachable.

Andrew and Mr. Wilson weren't at Eleanor's house.

"Please drop me off," Eleanor said with a yawn. "I think I ate too much ice cream. I'm sleepy."

"Is there such a thing as too much ice cream?" I yawned myself. "I'm heading home myself, and I don't care if Andrew is there or not. I'm so piling into bed."

<hr />

I filled my travel mug with coffee. I barely remembered Andrew coming home last night or to bed. He wasn't there when I woke, which was puzzling. It was so unlike my Andrew to not touch base. I really missed my husband.

I picked up Eleanor, who carried her own travel mug as she hopped in the car.

"Great minds," I said. "Is Mr. Wilson home?"

"Your Andrew and my Mr. Wilson went out on Captain Hamilton's charter boat to go fishing today."

"Hamilton certainly has been busy of late. It's no wonder Martha hasn't breathed a word about him," I said. Captain Hamilton was Martha's boyfriend, who ran a charter boat business in town. He gave up his position as captain of a cruise ship after he met my daughter. "I hope our husbands aren't planning to have us clean fish tonight."

Eleanor made a face. "Ew."

I drove to the hospital and we took the elevator to the third floor, where the coroner's office was located. There was no way they'd let us anywhere near the autopsy room, which under the circumstances I was okay with.

I knocked on the door and Walter Smitty opened it.

He smiled. "I expected you two yesterday. You're getting a little behind in your game."

"We knew yesterday would have been bad timing with the discovery of a body."

"You could say that when the state police were involved. I warn you, I haven't done the autopsy yet."

"That's fine. All we wanted to know is if the body is male or female," I said.

"And how long it's been in that barrel," Eleanor said.

Walter sighed as he interlaced his fingers. "I won't know the cause of death or how long it's been in the barrel. These things take time."

"Are the remains male or female?" I asked again.

"Female. And the sheriff informed me the remains might belong to a Faith Fleur. He has a search warrant for the room she's been staying at, so that will help with identification. Please be patient. I have enough pressure on me as it is. The sheriff is very concerned about the results of the autopsy and the implications."

I sighed. "I'm glad he's taking our findings seriously."

"I can't imagine him ignoring you two. You'd never give him a moment to sleep at night. Cases have a way of getting under the skin of law enforcement. They all want to find the killer."

"Faith hasn't been in the area that long, but she has taken up residence in town. I imagine Peterson would be concerned even if the victim was from out of town."

"That would be a travesty. Imagine what would happen if a tourist was found dead or murdered in Tawas? It would affect the entire county."

"I wouldn't look forward to that day," Eleanor said.

"Be careful ladies. I'll be in touch once I have some results. We won't tell the sheriff about that now, will we?"

"He won't hear it from me," I said and nudged Eleanor softly in the ribs.

"Me either," she chipped in.

※

WE SMILED WHEN I RAPPED ON THE DOOR OF PETERSON'S OFFICE. He glanced up from his paperwork and motioned us in with a wave.

"Close the door," he said, still focused on his papers.

I closed the door and Eleanor and I sat across from the sheriff. Papers were strewn across his desk, and stacks of paper were piled on top of manila folders.

Peterson's brows bunched. I wiped my hands on my slacks

nervously. It unnerved me that the sheriff had yet to speak. That couldn't be good, but at least he didn't refuse to see us.

He finally glanced up and leaned back in his chair. Large dark circles rimmed Peterson's eyes and his wrinkles were more pronounced.

"Are you feeling okay, Peterson?" I finally asked.

"Haven't slept all night." He inhaled sharply. "I can't get this case out of my head. Is it possible that a serial killer has been at work right here in our backyard?"

"Have you had any luck trying to find the case in which Wilber was a suspect?"

He shook his head. "No, and none of the enquiries I've made to the FBI have been returned." Peterson's eyes met mine. "I don't suppose you could give your son a call?"

I wiped more sweat off my palms. "I've been thinking the same thing. I hope he's not too heavily involved in a case right now. I'll tell him you're also involved so he'll move on it faster. I have a feeling he's annoyed when I bother him for privileged information."

"When has that ever stopped you before?"

"Good, so we're on the same page. I can't imagine Smitty has completed the autopsy yet."

Peterson sat back. "Is that what he told you?"

"I don't know what you're talking about, Peterson," Eleanor said. "We'd never go behind your back to talk to the coroner."

"Hah, that would be the day. In this case, though, I don't mind. It saves you from questioning me."

"He didn't give us any details, but he did tell us the victim was female, as we suspected. I only hope the body hasn't been there longer than we believe. Have you searched the property again?"

"Excavating will continue through the day."

"Have any more bodies been discovered?" Eleanor asked.

"I haven't received a call so far, and I hope that I won't."

"Let's all pray that won't be the case," I said.

CHAPTER 13

Eleanor and I were seated across from my son Stuart and his wife, Moraine, both of them FBI agents. We decided to meet at a family restaurant a few towns over that had a huge dining room. We were seated in the back, affording us lousy service but plenty of privacy.

Stuart sported a black eye and Moraine had a bandage on her brow.

"You're a sight for sore eyes," I said.

"Just another day in the life of FBI agents." Eleanor chuckled.

"It's embarrassing to admit a senior citizen beat the crap out of us," Moraine said.

Stuart shot his wife a look. "We're not here for shop talk."

"Oh, what's the matter," Eleanor asked. "It sounds like an interesting story. What were you busting him for, running a meth lab?"

"Eleanor," I warned.

"Doing a wellness check." Moraine smiled.

"The man was the father or our supervisory agent," Stuart said.

"That's understandable," I said. "If someone I didn't know showed up my house ... ."

"She'd call me to whip their you-know-what," Eleanor interjected.

"It's always good to have someone you can lean on," Moraine agreed.

"Let's get back to why we've called you here today," I said. "I'm really happy that you both could meet with us."

Moraine, a vibrant brunette, nudged my muscular son with a flirty look.

Stuart put his hands on the table. "What do you want, Mother? And please don't waste our time telling me we're assembled here to catch up."

"Don't talk to your mother like that," Moraine scolded.

"Fine, I'll keep it short," I said. "I'm investigating a case and we've found out that the murder victim might have been —."

"We're investigating the case," Eleanor interjected.

I sighed. "Getting back to particulars." I narrowed my eyes at Eleanor. "The victim is the ex-husband of one of our friends."

"Oh no! Who?" Moraine asked, ignoring Stuart's rolling eyes.

"Bernice. You might remember we called her The Cat Lady in the past."

"I'll bet that's putting her in the sheriff's crosshairs."

"Yes, but we've ruled her out. I'm not here to discuss the case exactly, but the victim's daughter mentioned her father was a suspect in a string of murders when she was younger."

"Specifically missing hitchhikers," Eleanor added.

Stuart exchanged a look with Moraine and she quickly pulled out a notebook. "How old is the daughter?"

"I'd say late twenties."

"We'll head to back to Tawas with you," Stuart said. "I'd like to speak to the daughter."

"It will help us determine what year we'll need to begin our search," Moraine added.

"Mentioning hitchhikers makes me think of crimes that might have occurred in the sixties or seventies," I said. "I don't think women hitchhiked in the nineties, and they certainly don't now."

"Which is why we'd like to question Bernice's daughter," Stuart said. "What's her name?"

"Callie Riley," I said. I then brought Stuart and Moraine up to date on the case thus far.

"You found a body stuffed in a barrel on Wilber's property?" Stuart asked in shock.

"Yes. And a bloodstain on the carpet in his house."

"So you believe that Wilber was a suspect in the murders of the hitchhikers?"

"We believe someone might have found out where Wilber was living."

"And took their revenge," Eleanor added.

"Sounds like a complicated case," Moraine nodded. "Has the body on the property been identified yet?"

"No, but we learned it's a woman," I said.

"It has to be Faith Fleur. The last time anyone saw her was two weeks ago," Eleanor said.

"I get killing Wilber, but why Faith?" Stuart asked.

"That's what we're trying to find out."

"I'm skeptical about the missing hitchhikers, but we'll take a look at the open cases."

"And cases that involve missing young women," Eleanor added.

※

ELEANOR AND I PACED THE CONFINES OF THE HALLWAY AT THE motel where Callie and Angelo were staying. Stuart refused to allow us in on the conversation with Wilber's children. And for once I let it go. I needed Stuart and Moraine's take from the perspective of FBI agents.

"Do you think it's possible that Wilber had been killing young women when he was married to Bernice?" Eleanor asked me.

"I'd rather not think about it."

"He certainly had his issues back then."

"We've already established he had an affair with another woman," I said. "But if he was a monster, why would he press for custody?"

"Maybe Bernice really wasn't in any condition to take care of the children," Eleanor said.

"I can't imagine what it will do to Bernice if she finds out she was married to a monster all those years."

"If you remember, the seed has already been planted with Bernice."

I pumped coins into a pop machine that looked like it was from the seventies. The plastic cover had tape holding the sign together, but at least it worked, and I grabbed the can that clattered from the machine. I held it against my hot face when Stuart and Moraine joined us.

"We have the necessary information," Stuart said. "We'll be heading back to the office to sort this out."

"Don't give up on your end," Moraine said. "We might not find out anything useful."

"She's right, but it's certainly worth checking out."

"I just love it when you say I'm right," Moraine said. "It makes me warm and giddy inside."

Stuart's brow furrowed. "I'll give you a call if I learn anything," Stuart said.

We walked Stuart and Moraine to their car. "So what did you think of Callie and Angelo?" I asked Stuart.

"They're upset, not that I blame them. If someone told me that my late father was a serial killer I don't think I'd take it well either," Stuart said. "Do yourself a favor and leave them alone. There's a lot that can be said about loose surveillance."

"So we want Wilber's children to relax enough to make a wrong move?" I asked.

"It's been known to happen." Stuart shrugged. "It wouldn't hurt to change up vehicles either."

"I knew there was a reason I called you," I said.

CHAPTER 14

I met Andrew in the sheriff's department parking lot as arranged when I'd called him. He was standing by his Lexus LX when Eleanor and I clambered out of Martha's station wagon.

"Thanks for meeting us, Andrew," I said.

His brow furrowed. "So lay it on me."

"Stuart and Moraine were in town, but they had to leave to check out a cold case." I then told Andrew the specifics about what Stuart and Moraine were looking into.

"And you two think someone waited until now to exact their revenge?"

"It's worth checking into."

"Is that it?"

"Stuart mentioned it might be a good idea if Eleanor and I did a little surveillance," I said.

"We're going to follow Bernice's children," Eleanor added.

"And my son thought it might be a good idea to change vehicles. I hope you don't mind if we take the LX."

"And drive what exactly?"

"Your ride awaits you," I said with a sweep of my arm toward Martha's station wagon.

"Where is your Mustang?"

"Martha is still driving it. It's much too small for Eleanor and me."

"I suppose you're right. And I'm too tall to sit in it comfortably. I'd also need a pry bar to get Mr. Wilson out of it."

"So we're good?"

"Of course, dear! Please be careful," Andrew said, exchanging keys with me.

I gave him a quick kiss before Eleanor and I were on our way. We headed back to the motel and the sedan that Callie and Angelo had been driving around town. It was still parked outside of Room ten. Fortunately there was a motel across the road from which we could conduct our stakeout.

Eleanor moved the back of her seat down slightly and yawned. "How about you watch and I take a nap?"

"Perhaps moving the seat back is a good idea; less conspicuous."

The traffic going to and from Tawas was sparse at best, allowing us a perfect view. I wished we'd brought a cooler. We could have filled it with soda and snacks of the candy bar variety.

"Are we going to see Bernice later today?" Eleanor asked.

"She's at Elsie's house, remember?"

"That's what I mean. Do you actually believe Bernice and Jack will get along?"

"Jack is Elsie's problem. Honestly, I don't know if Bernice and Jack have ever mingled socially."

"Besides Elsie's card parties, you mean."

"Elsie hasn't had as many of those of late," I said.

"It's too bad. I really looked forward to them," Eleanor said.

"Things have certainly changed since we got married."

"Well, that and Jack being on a diet. And now Bernice had a stroke. It has me thinking about my own mortality."

I shifted in my seat to look at Eleanor. From the somber expression on her face I knew she was serious. "I'd rather not think about it and live my life. Handle medical issues as they arise."

"We could drink less soda and watch what we eat more. Maybe even incorporate more salads in our diet."

I swallowed hard. "I wouldn't mind eating salads, but I don't want one for my last meal. Dr. Thomas suggested I lose a little weight and cut the fats, but the medication has brought my cholesterol down."

"I know I'm much bigger than you, but I don't even have high blood pressure. Maybe I'm thinking too much about what happened to Bernice."

"She pulled through fine."

"Let's hope it stays that way."

"Ouch!" I hissed when I slammed my knuckles on the steering wheel. "The suspects are on the move."

I repositioned my seat and cruised onto 23, following Angelo and Callie's car toward Tawas from a distance. I swung into the Walmart parking lot when Angelo went through the McDonald's drive-through and waited until they were back on the road. They headed up 55, and I followed suit. When they slowed so did I until they sped up. I lost them for a moment until I had an idea.

"I bet they're heading to their father's house," I said.

"But it's a crime scene. They must be up to something."

We passed Wilber's house. The crime scene tape had been breached and car tracks led to the back of the house. I continued up the road before turning around and pulling into Robert Boyd's driveway.

"What are we doing here?" Eleanor asked.

"We can almost see Wilber's house from here, and I believe if we use the binoculars ... we might be able to see the car Bernice's children are driving in the back yard."

Eleanor pulled out the binoculars and I used them to spy on Wilber's house.

"Um, I hate to bother you, Agnes, but Robert is standing on his porch watching us."

I put the binoculars in Eleanor's big black purse and we walked to meet Robert on his porch.

"Hello," I greeted. "I hope we didn't come at a bad time."

"Looks to me that you're trying to spy on Wilber's house, not pay me a visit."

"Not true," I said.

"There's been an unexpected development in our investigation," Eleanor said. "Could we come inside and talk with you about it?"

"Might as well since you came all the way here."

Eleanor and I sat on the couch Robert pointed to. He sat opposite us in a leather recliner. I glanced out his picture window. He had the perfect view of Wilber's property.

"You have a good view of Wilber's house from here," I said.

"I suppose you're right. It's been busy over there the last few days. I've never seen so many cops coming and going. And with heavy equipment."

"What do you suppose they're looking for?" Eleanor asked.

"Whatever it is, must be important."

"Did you happen to notice the sedan that pulled in over there?" I asked.

"Yup. Who you suspect it is?"

"His children are in town. Probably one of them."

"Shouldn't be crossing the crime scene tape."

"I know. We got into trouble with the sheriff for doing just that," I said.

"So you're the ones who stirred things up."

"I don't understand."

"First you two go snooping around over there, and then the cops show up like flies on hot garbage. What's really going on over there?"

"We found a body."

"A body? Who?"

"I don't have a clue. We were hoping you had more information than you told us the last time."

Robert gritted his teeth. "I don't know what you mean."

"Agnes, would you quit harassing the man," Eleanor asked. "We heard that Wilber might have been suspected of a murder."

"We can't keep this from Robert. He has the right to know the truth," I said. "And it's murders, not a murder."

Robert flopped back in his chair. "What murders?"

"We don't know exactly, but word has reached us that he was suspected in the disappearances of female hitchhikers years ago."

Robert massaged his stubbled chin. "How long are we talking here?"

"That's what we're trying to figure out," Eleanor said.

"We think it was when Wilber's children were much younger."

"Wilber has lived here only five years."

It was my turn to fall back, which was basically an act for Robert's benefit. I knew Wilber hadn't lived in Tawas long. "It appears we might have made a big mistake."

"Don't get too hasty now. You said you found a body over there besides Wilber's. That must mean something."

"You're quite perceptive," I said.

"I was an insurance investigator. It comes with the territory."

"I was thinking you were a cop or PI."

"You'd be shocked how many phony insurance scams there are."

I handed Robert our card. "Give us a call if you can think of anything else. Wilber's ex-wife is a good friend of ours."

"Wilber was leading her to believe they'd get back together, I think," Eleanor said. "She said he was acting strange before his disappearance. She didn't know he was dead in his house all that time."

"Way it sounds, there was more to Wilber than any of us thought," Robert said. "You'll get a better view of Wilber's place from inside with those binoculars."

"Sounds like something you know a lot about," I said.

I glanced through the binoculars and sighed when I didn't notice Angelo's car. "Seems we missed him."

"I wouldn't be so sure, but you might be able to flush them out. Call the cops and tell them someone is lurking around over there."

"But what if they're not?"

"Only way you'll know. If you drive in the driveway they'll know you're spying on them."

"I wonder why they'd be over there," I said. "It just seems strange because they're considered suspects. You notice Wilber's children over there a few weeks before he was murdered?"

"Like I told you earlier, the black SUV is the only vehicle I saw over there."

"Do you know Faith Fleur? Supposedly she was the one over to Wilber's."

"She delivers groceries for Neiman's," Eleanor added.

"She could be a suspect too," Robert said.

"We thought so, but she's nowhere to be found. She hasn't been seen for two weeks."

"You think she's dead?"

"We don't know yet. We're waiting for the coroner to identify the body."

"I don't envy you ladies. I never had to investigate a murder, although there was a man who faked his own death. He had a sizable life insurance policy that was paid to his widow. Poor woman had no idea her husband wasn't dead after all. She had to pay all the funds back. It was a sad case."

"How awful," Eleanor said.

I called the sheriff, who promised to have a deputy check out Wilber's property. Eleanor and I thanked Robert and left.

CHAPTER 15

Eleanor and I waded through cats when we arrived at Elsie's house. Apparently a provision of Bernice coming here to stay involved allowing her to bring her cats.

The cats parted and weren't nearly as aggressive as they were when at Bernice's house. Of course, I could imagine they were territorial there and now they didn't know what was going on.

Elsie waved us inside the door. We had to slide in to prevent one of the cats getting inside.

"It was right kind of Elsie to allow Bernice to bring her cats here," Rosa Lee said as she reclined on the rocking chair with a glass of lemonade.

Elsie bristled. "I did no such a thing."

"My cats are better than any watchdog, you'll see," Bernice said from a card table where she sat with Jack. "We're playing dice."

"We're in the middle of a game," Jack said. "She has me by two-thousand points and I'm about to win the game."

"Not when I roll a five-hundred," Bernice replied.

"I wouldn't get in the middle of them two. They've been at it since Bernice arrived." Elsie laughed. "And here I was worried they wouldn't have anything in common."

"It shouldn't have been too much of a stretch. We all like to play cards and dice," Rosa Lee said, taking a sip of lemonade.

"We weren't expecting to see you today, Rosa Lee," I said.

She shrugged. "Beats cleaning up spit."

I almost choked. "Spit?"

"Yup. Those boys of mine behaving like fools on account of the girl." She shook her head. "You need a boarder?"

"I hardly think she'd want to stay with an old couple like Andrew and me."

"No men to flirt with," Eleanor added with a snicker.

"Flirting is one thing, but if I don't get Gia to move on she might get in the family way and we'd be drawing straws to figure out which of my lughead sons are responsible."

"Don't you want to be a grandmother?" Bernice asked with a grin.

Rosa Lee shot her a look. "I'm going to forget you said that. I love my boys, but neither of them are father material. They can barely remember to put the seat up when they pee."

"I'm with Rosa Lee," I said. "The day we were at your place we caught her in the woods with Curtis."

"We almost caught them doing more than kissing," Eleanor added.

"They were by the old cabin," I said.

"I always knew I should have had it torn down," Rosa Lee said.

"We spotted your boys with the girl at Marion's."

"That time Gia was hanging all over Curt." Eleanor laughed.

"You better get those sons in line," Jack said. "She's trying to get her hooks into them."

"And break up your family," I added.

"If it comes to that, Gia will have to get packing. My boys mean too much to me."

"I can't see them letting a woman get between them."

"And definitely not between you and them," Eleanor said.

"If anyone has any ideas I'd love to hear them," Rosa Lee said.

"Don't interfere or it will go against you, Rosa Lee," Elsie said. "It's better in these situations to let them figure it out on their own."

"Ha," Jack said. "They'll move for sure then. You need to remind them of their responsibilities. Jimmy said they haven't come out to his place to help with his new house."

"New house?" Elsie asked.

"Jimmy is building it himself. He has the foundation poured," I said.

Rosa Lee narrowed her eyes. "What you been out to Jimmy's place for?"

"It involves our case."

"Did you find out who killed Wilber yet?" Bernice asked.

"We're not even close to a solid clue."

"What about what Callie said about my ex being a serial killer?"

I sank to the couch. "I have someone checking into that. We can't let Callie lead us astray when we don't even know if there is any truth to it."

Eleanor smiled slightly. "Do you think Wilber capable of something like that?"

"It's a hard question," Bernice said as she jotted down her score. "Callie said this was when she was younger."

"What if she was wrong? What if he was a killer when he was still married to you?"

"Agnes, I can't believe you," Elsie said. "Bernice is recuperating."

"Well, I don't know any other way to say it."

"No need to blame Agnes. I've been thinking about that. And Wilber was a salesman. He spent a lot of time away from home. He had plenty of opportunity."

"If he had a mind to do something that vicious," Eleanor said. "The sheriff had Wilber's property excavated. We don't know if any more bodies turned up."

"His place is still a crime scene, but we saw your children there today."

Bernice frowned. "I wonder what they're up to."

"I really want to think they're not involved, I mean this is their father," I began, "but what possible reason would they have to be over there when they know the investigation is in full swing?"

"It's their inheritance," Elsie insisted. "I bet they're just worried about the house being locked up."

"I wonder if Wilber had a will?" Eleanor said.

"Don't look at me," Bernice said. "Wilber didn't share that sort of information."

"Maybe you're right, Elsie, and they aren't up to no good."

"Other than throwing their own mother under the bus?" Eleanor grumbled.

"I don't trust either of my children," Bernice said with a shake of her head.

"I hope we haven't upset you. We really came here to see how you're doing," I said.

"You haven't made me any more upset than I already am. I won't feel safe until the murderer is found."

"Are you sure there wasn't anything Wilber might have said that could give us a clue?"

Bernice put her palms on the table. "He was acting distant, but I figured he wanted to end things between us."

"You told us there wasn't anything between you two."

"I didn't want the sheriff to know. He already thinks I'm capable of murdering Wilber."

"I think you need to go back to the beginning."

Bernice sighed. "We did go out, like I already told you, but we spent the night together a few times here and there."

Jack's eyes bugged out. "Why do tell Bernice!"

I glared at Jack as Bernice continued, "There wasn't anything debauched about it. When you get to by my age it feels good to have a man hold me. I didn't think I was that sort of woman, but I was wrong. I tried to fit the model of a woman he'd be interested in. But none of my fancy clothes could do that. I feel like such a fool now."

"Please don't," I said. "I won't share your admission with the sheriff."

"I told you the other part. He quit coming inside for coffee after he mowed my lawn. His visited less and less, and I was so hurt." Bernice wiped her tears with the back with her shirt tail. "Then I got angry, but I had too much pride to tell him to get lost. I started wearing my men's clothing again, but by then when Wilber came over he just sat in his truck."

"He had some demons," I said. "Whatever was happening in Wilber's life was huge. Too big for him to handle or to share with you, Bernice."

"Don't blame yourself," Eleanor said. "You didn't know what to do, like many of us. It's so easy to say you'd do this or that, but when confronted with a problem like that I can't say I would have done anything differently."

"Thank you, Eleanor. I appreciate my friends being here for me. All I can say is if Wilber was a serial killer when I was him I didn't know anything about it."

❦

ELEANOR AND I MADE AN UNEXPECTED APPEARANCE AT NEIMAN'S meat counter, where a robust woman greeted us. Her name badge read "Peggy."

"Hello ladies." She motioned to porterhouse steaks in the counter. "We just got a delivery of what I think are the leanest porterhouses you'll find in town."

"I believe that," I said. "You always have the best meat in town."

Eleanor nodded. "We're here to speak to the manager. I believe his name is Darrell."

"Darrell doesn't work her anymore. He's taken another job at the Harrisville Harbor Grocery."

"That seems sudden," I said. "He didn't mention that the last time we were here."

Peggy's brow arched sharply. "Do you know Darrell?"

Eleanor leaned on the meat counter. "Of course we know him. Otherwise why would we be here?"

Peggy shrugged.

"Do you know Faith Fleur?" I asked. When Peggy hesitated I said, "She delivers groceries for the store."

"I remember her."

"What can you tell us about her?"

Peggy glanced around as if to ensure that nobody could overhear her. "She was a little too friendly with Darrell before she pulled her disappearing act."

"Did the owner catch wind of it?" Eleanor asked.

"I can't speak for the owner, but I believe the only thing he didn't care about was the negative attention since Faith disappeared. Sheriff Peterson searched the SUV she used for deliveries. I think they found something, but I couldn't say what."

"Did the owner question Darrell about it?"

"I couldn't say. The tension was pretty high around the store until Darrell left."

"People in town no doubt wanted to hear every little detail," I said.

"Exactly."

"Faith is believed to be missing," Eleanor said somberly.

Peggy sighed. "I hoped that wouldn't be the case."

Eleanor swiped her hand across the top of the meat counter and looked at her dust-free fingers. "Did Darrell appear upset when Faith didn't come to work?"

"Not in the least."

"Seems like he'd be upset if an employee suddenly didn't show up to work. I imagine people were counting on having their groceries delivered."

"He's a manager. They never let us see them sweat," Peggy insisted.

"Well, that is the professional way to act, but in our experience emotions are often hard to cover up when you're upset," I said. "Is the owner here? I'd like to speak to him."

"Neiman's is run by the children of the original owners, and they're in Florida for a conference. It's been a few months since they've been in the store."

"If that's the case then how did you know the owners didn't care for the negative attention?"

"If you owned the store wouldn't you feel that way?"

"I suppose so, but I don't think Neiman's has gathered any negative attention. The cops searched a company-owned vehicle, not the store," Eleanor said.

"A vehicle, I might add, driven by an employee presumed missing.

Anything Faith may have been doing before her disappearance has no reflection on Neiman's. Thank you for your time, Peggy," I said.

Eleanor and I purchased a few fresh doughnuts before leaving the store. The wind felt great and Tawas Bay was spectacular. Seagulls were fishing on the bay instead of begging for food in picnic areas.

I drove north and swung into the sheriff's department.

"I thought we'd be heading for Harrisville," Eleanor said.

"Not quite yet. I'd like to find out what Peterson has to say about the money they found."

"We found, you mean. I wonder whose money it is."

"I can't imagine it belongs to Neiman's. It would have hit the airwaves with a resounding clap."

"She delivered groceries," Eleanor reminded me. "The orders were paid by credit or debit cards, remember?"

"Of course the person who told us that left town."

"Still, I can't imagine them handling it any other way."

Peterson stopped dead in his tracks when we ran across the parking lot to catch up to him.

"Thanks for waiting for us, Peterson," I said. "We have something important to talk to you about."

"It will have to wait until I get back. I have important business to take care of."

We nodded and watched as he tore out of the parking lot and threw the sirens on.

"Where do you think he's going?" Eleanor asked.

"I don't know, but we're about to find out."

By the time we were back on the road Peterson was nowhere to be found ... and the road to Wilber's house was blocked with police cars.

"This isn't good."

"What are we going to do now?"

"Head to Harrisville and find Darrell."

"Shouldn't we find another way to get to that road?"

"We'll check it out when we get back. Things might be calmed down by then or at least the road might not be blocked. I don't want to tangle with Peterson right now."

"I would have thought he'd have at least hinted where he was going," Eleanor grumbled.

"He knows if he did that we'd never leave him alone."

"You're probably right. Onward, James."

CHAPTER 16

I adjusted the seat to a more comfortable position. I enjoyed driving the LX. The leather seats felt cool and the air conditioning could freeze your nose. I almost felt bad for Andrew as the AC in Martha's station wagon simply does not exist. The seats were frayed, requiring several afghans to cover the springs. Forget about power anything, I'm shocked that the windows even roll down.

"Do you think Darrell is involved in Wilber's murder?" Eleanor asked.

"I'd love to know what his deal is. It's awfully convenient that he sent us on a wild goose chase and now doesn't work at Neiman's anymore."

"You're right about that. He lied to us -- and I hate liars!"

"Almost as much as I hate murderers, especially when one of my friends is a suspect," I said.

"I don't think anyone believes that anymore," Eleanor said. "Except maybe her children."

"I don't see how Bernice could have such rotten children. I swear they murdered their own father to get their own mother thrown in jail for the murder."

"That sounds like a motive. They haven't forgiven her for not being in their lives when they were children -- and it wasn't even her fault."

"They don't believe Bernice at all -- or us. Maybe Wilber was a serial killer. He certainly knew how to manipulate his own children."

"I hope Stuart finds something on that end soon. I'm beginning to think this is really what is happening here," Eleanor said. "The whole thing was set up, but if Wilber was really a serial killer and a victim's family found out, why kill him instead of turning him into the police?"

"Because it's too personal. They wanted to see him die."

I drove to Harrisville not knowing what to expect from Darrell. Would he tell us the truth or his version of the truth? Was he responsible for Faith's disappearance?

We passed Oscoda and as we continued north trees packed closer to 23, opening only for the sporadic motels dotting the highway. I imagined an era in which these motels were all filled despite not being near Lake Huron. Times were easier back then, and campgrounds were always crowded.

HARRISVILLE IS A VERY SMALL TOWN WITH A WONDERFUL STATE PARK and even lovelier beach. I pulled up to the Harrisville Harbor Grocery. It buzzed with activity.

A woman greeted us as she handed out samples of Cuban pork cutlets. "We have Chef Martin with us today, and you'll love what he's cooked up for us." She sliced the cutlet and set it on small paper plates. Eleanor and I eagerly took a sample and a plastic fork. From the way Eleanor looked down at her plate I knew she was about to say the sample was much too small, so I guided her to the rear of the store.

Eleanor was plastered to the glass, gazing at the cooked cutlets, mashed potatoes, green beans and every other variety of prepared food. We eagerly purchased a cutlet dinner for $6.99 and carried our Styrofoam containers to the meat counter, where we were told we'd find the manager.

"Hello there," I greeted the short man who worked behind the counter. We could barely see his eyes from where he stood.

"We're here to speak with the manager," Eleanor said. "Darrell."

"Darrell isn't the name of the manager."

"We were told he left Neiman's for a position here," I said.

"I'll get the manager."

The short man disappeared through a sliding door and a woman motioned us back. "Let's talk in my office."

When we were sitting in the office the woman interlaced her fingers. "I was told you were looking for a man named Darrell."

"That's right. He was a manager at Neiman's."

"Ah, well, we did hire a manager from Neiman's, but he didn't work out."

"That quick?"

"His credentials didn't check out."

"But he was a manager at Neiman's Family Market."

"I'm not certain how he managed to work there when Darrell isn't his real name."

"I'd appreciate it if you could give us his real name. We're investigating a missing person."

"His real name is Earle Richards. He has a criminal record for fraud. That's all I can tell you."

"Do you have any idea how we could find him?"

"I'll give you the address he put on his application."

❧

I RAPPED ON THE DOOR OF A DISMAL CABIN ON 23. IT APPEARED THE cabin hadn't been refinished or maintained in many years.

Eleanor's hand went to her hip as if she was packing as the door opened a crack. All I could see was a very wide blue eye and a swatch of blond hair.

My eyes widened. "We know who you are," I said.

"And unless you want us to call the police, you might want to open the door," Eleanor threatened.

The door opened further. Darrell stood behind the woman. She backed up. "I don't understand. I haven't done anything wrong."

"If you're Faith Fleur you have some serious questions to answer," I shot back. "We were led to believe you're a missing person."

"Sheriff Peterson will be very interested in this development," Eleanor said as she folded her arms across her ample chest.

"You don't understand. I had to go into hiding."

"Why so suddenly?"

"Please, nobody can know where I'm at."

"Give me one reason why," I said. "I'm a reasonable woman."

"No you're not," Eleanor whispered. "Neither of us are."

I didn't have time to glare at Eleanor. I was reading the expression that drifted across Faith's face as her lips turned into a frown. "You won't understand."

"Leave her alone," the man we had known as Darrell said. "She doesn't have to answer your questions."

"She does if she doesn't want the cops showing up. She's cost Iosco County serious money investigating her disappearance."

"You don't understand," Darrell said.

"Does Faith know you're real name isn't Darrell and that you've had several brushes with the law?"

"Who told you that?"

"The manager at Harrisville Harbor Grocery. You know, the one who did a background check on you, Earle."

"I have a twin brother and he's the one with the criminal background. His name is Earle. People get us confused all the time."

"And I suppose your social security numbers are the same too," Eleanor said with a sneer. "Or driver licenses?"

Darrell rubbed the nervous sweat from his face. "Earle used my identification when he was arrested for fraud. I thought I had cleared it up, but apparently that's not the case. I'll have to hire an attorney, but it will be hard to do without a job."

"Why did you quit Neiman's?"

"I didn't have a choice, not with you two on my case about Faith. You even managed to get Sheriff Peterson snooping around."

"Leaving town makes you appear suspect," I said. "Things like this just don't go away."

"You knew your lie about Faith would come back to haunt you," Eleanor added with a curt nod.

"What lie?" Faith asked meekly.

"That you went to Oscoda to take care of a sick aunt. Ellen Brighton."

"Except that Ellen is in very fine form, and you were supposed to have house sat for her while she was downstate. Why did you tell Bunny Vaverick you'd house sit for Ellen and then tell her you couldn't?"

Faith bit her lip. "After I found Wilber dead I knew I had to leave town. I didn't want my name mixed up in his murder."

"Ah, so you know he was murdered -- at least that's something."

"You found him dead two weeks before his body was discovered." Eleanor gasped. "And you just let his remains sit there decomposing while you made your escape?"

Faith clenched her small hands into bony fists. "I didn't have a choice. Whoever killed him might come after me."

"How can you be so sure?"

"Wilber wasn't the only one murdered in that house. There are bloodstains on the carpet."

"Yes, we saw the one in the living room."

"No, I mean before that. There was a sizable stain on the carpet under the couch."

Eleanor tapped her foot, nearly rattling the salt and pepper shakers on the nearby kitchen table. "And when, pray tell, was that?"

Faith's brow wrinkled. "About three months ago."

"Why were you there?"

Darrell jumped into the conversation. "I told you —."

"You had your two cents," Eleanor said. "We want to hear what Faith has to say."

"I delivered Wilber groceries."

"So you spotted a bloodstain on the carpet when you delivered the groceries, but continued to come back," I said. "That's doesn't sound very believable. Would you go back to a house where you noticed bloodstains on the carpet, Eleanor?"

"Not a chance, but I would have called the police and reported it."

"I didn't think about that. You can't just go around trying to report everyone who has stains on their carpet. Wilber had the carpet replaced before I made my delivery the next week."

I massaged my chin. "What sort of groceries did Wilber have you deliver?"

"Vegetables. He was a vegetarian … and cleaning supplies. He must have been a germaphobe because he bought a lot of bleach."

"Or a serial killer," Eleanor said. "What else would explain bloodstains on his carpet and a body disposed of in a barrel on his property?"

Faith laughed. "I don't see Wilber as a serial killer. He was too meek."

"Then why mention the previous bloodstains on his carpet?"

"Wilber has a son who is rather nasty. Now I can believe he's a serial killer."

"Angelo?"

"That's him."

"Is there a reason you're trying to deflect the thought that Wilber is a serial killer onto his son?"

Faith bit her lip. "I don't know what you want me to say."

"Angelo doesn't live in Tawas," Eleanor clarified. "So how could he be the killer?"

"He visited his father frequently -- almost every weekend."

"And his sister?" I asked.

"Wilber mentioned she comes about once a month."

"What was really going on with Wilber? Were you two personally involved?"

"No!" Faith exclaimed.

"Then why are you so quick to deny the possibility of Wilber being a killer?"

"I just don't understand how you can think that he was if he's been murdered himself."

"We have plenty of possibilities about that," Eleanor said. "But it sounds more likely that someone who had access to Wilber's house is the killer. And as it stands, you're the only one who did."

"The tow truck driver was at his house once."

"We're friends with Jimmy, and believe me, he's no killer."

"The only thing Jimmy kills is the money in your wallet if you don't have road service." Eleanor chuckled.

"Darrell told us you were the only one who used the SUV at Neiman's for deliveries." I said.

"I suppose."

"He assured us that was the case."

"That's right," Darrell said, "but where are you going with this?"

"Where did the cash we found in the SUV come from, Faith?"

Faith's eyes widened. "What cash?"

"A McDonald's bag full of wadded-up cash," Eleanor said. "We found it in the SUV."

"I might have taken that SUV for deliveries, but I don't know anything about cash in a McDonald's bag. Someone is trying to set me up."

"We've been all concerned about your disappearance. We believed your remains were in the barrel we found."

"I don't know what more I can say to assure you that I didn't have anything to do with Wilber's murder."

"I'm sorry, but we all need to go back to Tawas. Sheriff Peterson will be very interested in these developments."

CHAPTER 17

Sheriff Peterson sighed when I filled him in about Faith, who was sitting in one of his interview rooms. "I'm glad to hear that Faith isn't missing, but who is the woman you found in the barrel?"

"I don't know, but it sure appears that Wilber had some dark secrets, ones that might have led to his death," Peterson said. "Get back with your son, Agnes. I'd like to know if he's found out anything about those missing hitchhikers."

"I can't believe Faith found Wilber's body and didn't report it," I said.

"Don't worry, I'll sort it out. Let me just say that both Darrell and Faith will be my guests for at least the next twenty-four hours. Hopefully by then I can find out Darrell's real identity. I've heard the 'my twin stole my identity' story more than a few times."

"It sounded like a stretch to me too, but apparently the owners of Neiman's seemed to believe Darrell was exactly who he claimed to be."

We followed the sheriff to the interview room. "You two have been very helpful, but I'll be taking over now," Peterson said.

I smiled. "We know that, but where were you off to earlier? Your deputies had the road Wilber lived on blocked off."

"We had a report that a light was on in Wilber's house."

"We saw Wilber's children on the property."

"Well, they weren't there when we checked out the place. I had the house boarded up, so that should deter anyone from getting back inside."

"I thought you'd already done that."

"Apparently not good enough. I had extra boards put up to cover the patio door."

"Oh, that's good." I forced a smiled as I frowned on the inside. That would also keep us out of the house.

"Have you figured out where that money came from yet, Peterson?" Eleanor asked.

"Not yet, but hopefully Faith is in a talking mood."

"Good luck. We certainly couldn't get anything out of her," I said.

At least someone else wasn't killed at Wilber's house," Eleanor said when we were back on the road.

"I thought that too when the road was blocked off like that. Well, that or a fire. Crime scenes have been known to be set on fire."

"That would complicate matters for us if we wanted to break into Wilber's house."

"I'm glad we're friends, Eleanor. You're downright dangerous."

"I'm not saying we'd do it for real, but you never know." She grinned.

I pulled into the motel where Bernice's children were staying. Callie answered the door and let us inside.

Angelo sat on one of the beds with a noticeable frown. "So what brings you by?"

I plopped down on the only chair. "We have a few more questions."

"Why did you let them in, Callie?"

"Because I want to find out who murdered our father. And if it takes a few more questions from them, I'm willing to suffer through them."

The motel room was sparsely furnished, with two full-sized beds, a small television and a night table between the beds. It was apparent that Wilber's children were keeping expenses low while they were in town.

"It's too bad you can't stay at your father's house," I said.

Callie's face paled. "I don't think I'd care to stay there after the way our father was murdered."

"You should be kinder to your mother. She might allow you to stay at her house."

"I don't see that happening," Callie said. "Not since her medical scare."

"You mean mini-stroke," Eleanor said with cocked brow.

"Is this why you're here?" Angelo asked in irritation.

"We couldn't help but notice you were at your father's house since his murder," I said. "I couldn't help but wonder why."

"We wanted to see the damage the police did to the property. When everything is settled we'll have to sell the place."

I suppose that was right, but hearing Angelo say that had me thinking. "Did your father store any cash at his house?"

Angelo laughed. "Cash no. Plenty of bills, though."

"So you admit you went into the house, possibly turned on a light?" Eleanor asked.

"We did, but there wasn't a need to turn on the lights. We could see where we were going thanks to the sheer curtains," Angelo said. "Why?"

"With the windows boarded up? Unless you removed a few to gain entrance into the house," Eleanor said.

"You probably should have covered your tracks and put the boards back up," I said. "Sheriff Peterson went out to the house today after someone reported seeing a light. He had the house boarded up."

They both widened their eyes.

I stood and stretched, giving the chair to Eleanor. "One last question. We finally caught up to the woman who delivered groceries to your father. Apparently she wasn't missing after all. Anyway, she mentioned seeing a bloodstain on the carpet. We thought you might have something to say about it, Angelo," I offered.

"Why would I know?" he asked flippantly.

"The woman also told us you visited your father every weekend."

"Visiting your father every weekend isn't a crime. Most children rarely see their parents that much."

"As opposed to ignoring your mother."

"So you never noticed a bloodstain near the couch – or under it?" Eleanor asked.

"I hardly rearranged the furniture when I stopped by."

"What about the carpet being replaced? You have anything to say about that?"

"He might have had new carpeting installed, but Dad rarely threw anything out. I believe he might have laid the old carpeting on the basement floor. I imagine the sheriff could tell you more about the carpet than I can."

I helped Eleanor up. "Thank you again for answering our questions. I believe we'll find out who murdered your father soon."

❧

"Is it true that we're close to finding the killer?" Eleanor asked once we were outside.

"We might be, but we'll need to tell the sheriff about the carpeting in the basement. For some reason I think he overlooked it."

"It might have been covered with junk. You know that's how most basements are if they're not finished."

My phone rang and Stuart's voice came through the hands-free speaker. "Mother, drop whatever you're doing. I need to see you in Detroit."

"Is that really necessary?"

"Very."

"Why can't you tell me what you found out?"

"Believe me, you'll want to come here. I'm not at liberty to remove the information from the office."

"You win. We'll be there tomorrow morning."

CHAPTER 18

Andrew dropped us at the FBI's field office in Detroit, and Stuart walked out to greet us. He ushered us through the revolving metal door that was nearly too small for Eleanor's frame. We surrendered our identification to the security officer, who took our photos and placed them on guest passes. We then walked through the elaborate metal detectors and were patted down.

As we glided up the elevator, Eleanor and I refrained from speaking. I had to admit it was rather nerve wracking to be in the federal building, and from the look in Eleanor's eye I knew she felt the same.

We proceeded along the hallway when the elevator opened and into the records department. We made our way past row after row of locked file drawers that nearly reached the ceiling.

"Those contain hardcopies of documents," Stuart explained. "All the documents have been put into digital format and can be viewed from any office or at home." Stuart frowned. "You don't have access to do that, but I've been given permission for you to look over some of the missing persons cases pertaining to the missing hitchhikers," Stuart said.

I fished a small notebook from my purse and nodded as Eleanor and I followed Stuart into a side office with a large flat-screen attached to the wall. We sat around a half-moon table.

Stuart used a remote control to turn the monitor on and his fingers flew across a keyboard until the images of four young women came on the screen. Maggie Bauer, Brenda Meier, Dawn Wagner and Betty Driscoll. All of them had blond hair and blue eyes.

I quickly jotted down the names. "Could you give us some specifics?"

"What timeframe did the women disappear?" Eleanor asked.

"We were led to believe that Wilber was under investigation when his children were younger, which should make it about the late nineties or early two-thousands," I said.

Stuart shook his head. "What led you to believe that?"

"Wilber's daughter mentioned it, and she's about twenty-five."

"The cases Wilber was a suspect in occurred in 1976."

I bit the inside of my cheek. "I wonder if Bernice was married to Wilber at that time."

"We'll have to ask her when we get back to Tawas," Eleanor said.

"According to the files, Wilber Riley was twenty-eight when he came under suspicion," Stuart said.

"I'm not one-hundred percent certain, but Bernice must have been married to Wilber at that time," I said. "How exactly did he come under suspicion?"

"A white El Camino was spotted picking up female hitchhikers that resembled the missing woman on U.S. 23 between Greenbush and Alpena. Wilber owned the same model car."

"And worked as a traveling salesman there?" I asked.

"Yes, and he wasn't able to give a solid alibi at the time."

"If he worked in the area I imagine the police thought he was the likely suspect," Eleanor said. "In those days cops were hungry to place the blame."

Stuart's brow furrowed. "I don't believe that was the case with the FBI involved."

"Were the bodies ever found?" I asked.

"No. And believe me, the area was searched thoroughly."

"Why wasn't Wilber ever arrested?" Eleanor asked.

"He was taken in and questioned several times, but he wasn't the only suspect."

"Did the other suspects also drive same model as Wilber?" I asked.

"No, but that didn't make them any less suspect. Even if an El Camino was seen picking up hitchhikers, that doesn't mean it was the killer's vehicle. We have to assume at this point that the women are dead."

"So nobody was ever charged?"

"Peter Swiss confessed, but the details he gave didn't match what we know about the disappearances. He claimed he kidnapped and murdered the women in Grand Rapids."

"Maybe for another crime?"

"So I imagine the case went cold," Eleanor said.

"Whatever happened to the man who confessed?" I asked.

"Peter was killed by police during an armed robbery."

"In Grand Rapids?"

Stuart nodded.

"When was Wilber no longer considered a person of interest?"

"Wilber was in the hospital when Betty Driscoll was reported missing."

"So he was taken off the suspect list."

"Not exactly, but his name certainly dropped to the bottom of the list. Has the coroner been able to identify the remains found in the barrel?"

"We were told it would take more time -- unless you could make a call for us."

"Walter Smitty knows his job. And from what Sheriff Peterson tells me, the coroner has a hard time telling either of you no."

Stuart handed us bottled water from a small refrigerator. I sighed as I took a drink.

"Have any of the victim's families continued an interest in the case?" I asked.

"Brenda Meier's family called the FBI every year for an update -- up until a few years ago. They developed a close bond with Special Agent Miller. He died a few years back."

"Do you know their names?"

Stuart typed again and said, "Lisa Spraggs. She lives in Standish."

I wrote down Lisa's address and sighed. "We appreciate your help. Maybe Lisa will be able to help us -- unless you have the names of other family members who are still seeking justice."

"That's all I have. I hope you'll share any information you get from Ms. Spraggs. Please tell her we're still working the case. I only wish there was more we could do to find the killer."

"The person responsible might be dead by now," I suggested.

"Maybe that's why missing hitchhikers are no longer reported," Eleanor added.

I nodded. "Or the killer simply moved on."

"All good points, but none of them have brought the FBI closer to finding the murderer," Stuart said.

"And they never found the bodies."

"No. And believe me, every time bone fragments are found they're processed carefully. We all care about this case. If Wilber was the killer, after all this time it might bring closure to the victims' families."

"As if having a family member ripped away from you will ever give you the closure you'd want," I said.

Andrew rented a car as he decided to stay behind in Detroit with Mr. Wilson, so Eleanor and I were able to take the LX to Lisa's house. I was more than a little anxious to find out what she had to say about Betty and the suspects.

✥

"LISA SPRAGGS?" I ASKED AS WE CAUGHT HER BEFORE SHE ENTERED her house. Apparently she had just come from the grocery store as she balanced four stuffed plastic shopping bags.

The woman set her bags inside before joining us on her porch. She hugged her frail frame. Her heavily-wrinkled skin and straggly gray hair wasn't what I expected at all. She was at least as old as us.

"Are you Betty Driscoll's sister?" I inquired.

Eleanor moved in to catch Lisa as she fainted, and I rushed to help my friend in easing Lisa to a bench on the porch. Eleanor exchanged a startled glance with me. "Now what do we do?"

I knocked on the door, hoping Lisa didn't live alone, but when it wasn't answered my hopes were dashed.

"Help me get her inside," I finally said.

Eleanor and I managed to carry Lisa inside and ease her down into the closest chair. While Eleanor went to fetch a glass of water, I fanned Lisa's face with a magazine I found in the newspaper rack.

Eleanor flicked drops of water on Lisa with a shrug, "What? I don't have any smelling salts."

I leaned down and said, "Lisa, can you hear me?"

Eleanor sat next to Lisa and rubbed the top of her hand. "Lisa, are you okay?" Eleanor said.

"I wonder if we should call an ambulance," I said.

"You might want to scat. I just called the cops," a young woman with large blue eyes said as she stood in the doorway.

"Cops?" My hands slipped to my hips. "I know this might look strange, but Lisa fainted. We couldn't just leave her on the porch."

"We had no idea how fragile she was," Eleanor added.

The woman's brows knitted. "She's not normally. Didn't you just hear me tell you I called the cops?"

"I think calling an ambulance instead of cops would be better, don't you, young lady."

The woman walked into the kitchen and returned with an opened tiny bottle and waved it under Lisa's nostrils.

Lisa abruptly coughed and her eyes slowly opened. "What are you doing in my house?"

"That's what I thought. I called the cops."

"Oh, Denise I wish you hadn't gone and done that."

"You have intruders in your home."

I shook my head. "We most certainly didn't break into your house," I gasped.

"Agnes is right," Eleanor said. "Lisa opened the door. She even put her groceries inside, see." She pointed out the bags on the floor.

"I think we gave you quite the shock, Lisa."

Lisa blinked rapidly for a few moments. "Oh, it's coming back to me now. What did you say again that caused me to faint?"

"I'd rather not say if you reacted so strongly the first time," I said.

"We didn't come here to upset you. We were hoping to discuss Betty with you."

"Betty?" Denise asked in shock. "Did you find her remains?"

"Nothing like that. We're investigating a case in Tawas and we've learned the victim was considered a suspect in Betty's disappearance."

"Is this about Wil —."

"Yes, Wilber Riley," I said.

"No, that's not the name I was going to say, although I'm quite aware of the suspects that have been linked to my daughter's disappearance. I believe Wilson Conner was responsible for killing the missing hitchhikers."

"They haven't found their bodies," Denise reminded Lisa.

"No they haven't, but I feel deep in my heart that my Betty was murdered. The FBI believes that as well."

"My son is with the FBI," I said. "He's reviewing the files."

"You mentioned a Wilson Conner," Eleanor said. "Did the FBI give you that name?"

She nodded.

"How can they be so certain Conner killed the hitchhikers?"

"He confessed … on his deathbed."

"If that was the case, why is the FBI still looking at the case?"

"The FBI doesn't consider a deathbed confession all that reliable. They need to back it up with evidence."

My heart ached for Lisa. "From my understanding, you've kept up on the case every year until the last few years."

"That's right. I haven't contacted them since Wilson Conner died of cancer."

"How was he linked to the disappearances? Our sheriff told us Wilber was the seen on U.S. 23. He drove a white El Camino."

"Betty wasn't anywhere near 23. She hitchhiked on the west side of the state. She had friends who lived in Grand Rapids."

"Conner lived in Grand Rapids in those days," Denise said.

"What about the other girls?"

"I believe it was in the same area, which is what helped the FBI connect the cases."

My shoulders slumped. "So Wilber wasn't guilty after all," I sighed. "It appears that we've made a wrong turn in this case."

Cars skidded to a stop in front of the house and Lisa motioned whoever it was inside.

"What's the five-alarm all about this time," a muscular sheriff asked.

"This time?" Eleanor asked as her eyes narrowed. "Explain yourself."

The sheriff quickly apologized, "I didn't mean anything by that. It's just that Lisa just calls the cops more than most people in town."

"For your information, I didn't call, my daughter did," Lisa said. "These ladies helped me inside and Denise took it the wrong way."

"Should I call an ambulance for you?" the sheriff asked.

"I'm fine, as you can see."

"And we were just leaving," I said.

"Then I'd better get going too."

"Don't you dare, Sheriff Babble," Lisa said. "Denise, fetch a glass of lemonade for the sheriff."

"I can't stay," Babble protested.

"I know you love Denise's lemonade. It's fresh-squeezed."

Babble shifted nervously. "I suppose I have time for one glass, but if I get a call I'll have to leave."

Lisa winked at us.

Eleanor and I chuckled all the way back to the car. "I hope the sheriff knows what he's gotten into," I said. "I think Lisa wants Babble and Denise together."

"I can't blame Lisa for searching all these years for her daughter," Eleanor said.

I nodded. "It's what keeps cases open and law enforcement on their toes."

"Now that Wilber is cleared as a serial killer, whose remains did we find in that barrel?"

"Well, we'd better get back to town, because we certainly know it's not Faith."

CHAPTER 19

Eleanor and I sat across from Walter Smitty as his fingers raced along his keyboard. For some reason I hadn't expected him to type that fast. We were here to find out if the body found in a barrel on Wilber's property has been identified yet.

"Turns out the body is that of Faith Fleur. Congratulation, ladies, you called this one."

I frowned. "That's impossible. Faith Fleur is quite alive."

It was Smitty's turn to frown. "Perhaps you're wrong and the woman who you believe is Faith is not who you think she is. The state police were able to positively identify the victim from the fingerprint impressions I took during the autopsy. She was in the database."

"Thank you, Smitty," I called out as Eleanor and I ran from his office.

I gripped the steering wheel on the way to the sheriff's department.

"How about that," Eleanor began, "we should have known Darrell was lying."

"It wouldn't be the first time ... unless he really believes that's the name of the woman who was delivering groceries for Neiman's."

"Both of them are covering their true identities. Of course it's not every day that someone assumes the identity of someone who was murdered."

"Hopefully we'll be able to sort this out with the sheriff."

I pulled into a spot near the door and we caught up with the fake Faith and Darrell as they hurried to a vehicle. Eleanor called the sheriff for backup as I made a very unmovable barrier between the couple and their vehicle.

"Hello again," I said. "I'm so glad I caught you two before you left."

Faith sighed. "What are you talking about? I thought you were happy to find out I was alive."

"I was until I found out you're an impostor."

"Let's take this inside," Sheriff Peterson said as he joined us.

Eleanor and I followed the trio inside. I felt a little smug with Smitty's help.

The couple was split between two separate interview rooms. Peterson joined us in the observation area.

"So spill it," Peterson said.

"We've just come from Smitty's office."

Peterson's brow shot up. "I didn't receive his report yet."

"Neither did we, but the body has been identified," I said. "It's Faith Fleur."

"But we both know Faith is in that interview room."

"The fingerprints Smitty took were verified with the state police."

"That woman in the interview room is not Faith Fleur."

"We don't know who she really is," Eleanor said. "We didn't get the chance to find out her real identity."

"I thought you might want to handle that part. Peterson."

"You mean you're giving me permission to do my own job?" he smirked.

"We don't have a way to fingerprint her or the database to cross reference to see if she's in the system."

"I suppose you'd love to get a crack at questioning her?"

"Yes, but why don't we both question her?"

"Go ahead. I'll conduct my interview after you get what you need. I have other methods to get suspects to talk."

"Ah-ha," Eleanor said. "So you admit she's a suspect."

"I've been doing this job a long time. It seems that they're both using an assumed identity."

Eleanor nodded. "They must have both been involved with killing Faith and Wilber."

"The woman calling herself Faith already admitted that she found Wilber's body two weeks ago. I should have asked Smitty if he was able to determine how long Faith had been dead," I said.

"We'll sort that out at a later date," Peterson said.

"Are you going to take the woman's fingerprints before we talk to her?"

"No. We'll take her fingerprints off the glass of water I'm going to give her."

"Won't she wonder if you're trying to pull a fast one?" I asked.

Peterson's brow furrowed. "As if you bringing her one won't do that."

"Good point," Eleanor said.

We entered the interview room and Peterson set down a glass of water for the suspect. Eleanor and I sat opposite her as the sheriff left.

"Whew, it's really getting warm outside," I said. "I'm sorry we had to stop you outside, but we were given information from the coroner, which is why we're challenging your insistence that you're Faith Fleur."

"She's quite dead. Found in a barrel on Wilber's property," Eleanor added.

The woman's face fell. She covered her face with her hands and shook her head. She looked back up at us and said, "You think I killed Faith?"

"And Wilber," Eleanor said. "You did admit to finding his body, not that it matters, because you let his corpse rot for someone else to find."

"No, that's not what happened. I was given a message to go to Wilber's house."

I rolled my eyes. "Really, from who?"

"Does this have anything to do with the money we found in the SUV you were driving?" Eleanor asked.

"I don't know what you're talking about. What money?"

"We already told you about the money we found."

"Who were you meeting at Wilber's house?" I pressed.

"Why would you go to Wilber's to meet with someone anyway?" Eleanor asked.

"Just tell us who you are," I said. "We'll find out eventually, and it might go better for you."

"If you're as innocent as you claim to be," Eleanor added with a glint in her eye.

"This is all Darrell's doing. He called me and asked me to come to Tawas." She took a drink of the water. "He told me Wilber kept a large sum of money at home."

"So you went to Wilber's house to steal the money."

The woman swallowed hard. "And that's when I found Wilber's body."

"Did you find the money?"

"No. I wasn't about to search for the money with a dead body in the house. Someone might have dropped by."

"What about Faith?"

"She wasn't there."

"So you weren't the one who put her in a barrel?" Eleanor asked.

"How could I do that by myself? And why would I? Wilber was already dead and his body was obviously where he was killed. So why move Faith's body?"

"That's the part we're trying to work out," I said.

"Were you delivering groceries to Wilber?" Eleanor asked.

"No. Faith made deliveries. All he let me do is take the delivery vehicle to Wilber's house."

"He must have known Faith was missing," I said.

"Darrell set you up, from the sounds of it," Eleanor said. "He most likely killed Faith and had you use the delivery vehicle so your fingerprints would be found."

"Faith must have gotten in the way," I said. "Darrell couldn't have that."

"He only had me drive the black SUV so the neighbors wouldn't see anything out of the ordinary."

I laughed. "You had no idea that the money was in that vehicle the entire time."

"Spit it out, girl, what's you real name?" Eleanor ordered.

"Skye Shay. I'm sure the sheriff will find out I'm on probation for embezzlement."

"That was a big pill to swallow," I said. "So what priors does Darrell have?"

"Theft charges, but he's not on probation."

"Not that it will matter. You went to Wilber's house with the intention to steal from him. Were you planning to rob him?" I asked.

"Darrell assured me that he wouldn't be home on Wednesday."

"Is there anything else you'd care to share?" I asked.

"I suppose I won't be going anywhere."

"That will be up to the sheriff, but as you said, you're on probation."

"And went to Wilber's house to commit a crime," Eleanor said.

Eleanor and I left the room. "Well, it seems that Skye is your problem now, sheriff," I said. "We'd like to ask Darrell a few questions before we leave."

"Have you put anything together on your end yet?" Peterson asked.

"I'm hoping Darrell will give us something to go on because to be honest we're stumped."

"What did you find out from Stuart?"

"That Wilber was a suspect, but he's not good for the serial disappearances. One of the victim's family members told us her daughter was on the west side of the state, not hitchhiking on 23."

Peterson sighed. "I'm glad to hear that the person responsible doesn't live in Tawas."

"I concur. So are we okay to speak with Darrell?"

"Please do. I'll have a crack at Skye. Someone killed Faith, and she's already admitted that she was at Wilber's house. It still doesn't sit well with me that she found Wilber's body and didn't tell anyone."

❧

DARRELL'S EYES DARTED FROM US TO THE CAMERA POSITIONED IN the corner of the room. Both his arms had red marks on them. I watched as he scratched the inside of his arm. He was one nervous man. Of course, having a prior didn't help, and he did send Skye to Wilber's house to steal money.

Eleanor and planted our palms on the table and looked down at Darrell. I didn't say a word until I watched sweat surface on his upper lip.

"Hello, Darrell. We've already spoken to Skye. She told us the deal," I said.

Eleanor bared her teeth. "How did you know Wilber had money at his house?"

Darrell rubbed his palms over the corner of the table. "I heard it is all."

"From who?" Eleanor demanded.

"I don't know. I just overheard it."

"You overheard it or someone told you about it?" I asked.

"I go to Barnacle Bill's after work sometimes. Wilber's son hangs out there when he's in town. And we got to talking and he let it slip."

"He told you his father kept money in his house?"

"Yes. He was bitter about it because he was worried his father was funneling money to his mother but couldn't prove it."

"Did Angelo ever look for it?"

"No. He claimed the old man kept a good watch on him when he was there."

"For good reason, I'd imagine."

"Could be."

"So you called Skye and asked her to come to Tawas to steal the money?"

"I told her to go over there and take a look around. It's not like we were planning to rob the man."

"You make it sound like you were planning to do Wilber a favor by relieving him of his cash."

Darrell pursed his lips. "It sounds bad when you say it like that."

I laughed. "Really? Remind me not to run across the likes of either you or Skye."

"And for the record, neither of us keep cash at home," Eleanor added. "We don't even keep cash in the bank."

"Nope," I agreed. "We pay our bills with our money."

"Like honest people who make an honest living."

"Did you kill Faith?" I asked.

"No, you know that!" Darrell spat.

"I can't say we're even getting the whole story here."

"You didn't even know the money was hidden in the SUV all along." Eleanor chuckled. "You could have made it easier if you'd searched the SUV when Faith quit showing up for work."

"You know, you're right. What do you think is going to happen to us?" Darrell asked.

"You or Skye?" I asked. "She's on probation and I can't imagine she's leaving anytime soon."

Eleanor nodded. "Her probation will be revoked, most likely."

Darrell face palmed his head. "I wish Angelo had never told me that."

"Just because he told you his father kept money at home hardly gives you permission to take it from him -- unless Angelo was part of your scheme."

"He didn't have anything to do with it."

"We're off, Peterson," I said. "I hope you'll let us know Darrell's real name when you find out."

"I can do that right now -- Earle Richards. He spent time in prison for fraud in cases very similar to this one, without the dead body. At this point he looks good for murdering Wilber and Faith."

"And it's up to you to get a confession," I said. "I don't envy you."

CHAPTER 20

Eleanor knocked on the motel room door. Callie frowned when she opened the door, but she motioned us inside.

Angelo walked out of the bathroom, a towel draped over his shoulder.

"What now?"

"We have a few questions and we'll leave. I promise," I said.

Angelo shook his head in anger pelting us with drops of water from his wet hair.

"Let them talk," Callie said as she plopped down on the bed.

"Did your father keep a large sum of cash at his house?" I asked.

"I don't know if I'd consider it a large sum," Callie said. "He didn't trust his money in the bank. Never did."

Angelo's eyes widened. "Does this have to do anything with his murder?"

"Yes and no. Darrell, or I should say Earle, told us you told him your father kept money in the house," I said.

"Said you were worried that he'd given the money to your mother," Eleanor added.

Callie shot Angelo a look. "Really? I can't imagine that would ever happen."

Angelo's eyes widened. "She was trying to get close to him."

"We've already established that both your father and mother were getting closer of their own free will," I said. "I believe money was stolen from Wilber's house. We found cash in the vehicle that delivered groceries to him. Then Faith went missing around the same time, and someone murdered her at your father's house and hid her body in a metal barrel hidden near the shed."

"Nobody realized the money was hidden in the SUV the entire time," Eleanor added.

"Did Faith steal our father's money?" Angelo asked.

"I believe so, but that still doesn't explain who killed your father or why."

"He must have found out his money was missing," Callie offered. "He'd be quite angry about that."

"Do you think Wilber killed Faith, Agnes?" Eleanor asked. "It makes sense."

"No. I think someone else did it. He was acting strange. And there was the bloodstain on his carpet."

"That would do it for me, but I'd have called the police," Eleanor said.

"And say what? Wilber was a suspect in a string of missing hitchhikers," I said. "He's since been ruled out as a suspect."

"I'm glad to hear that," Callie said. "So where is this Earle now?"

"Being questioned at the sheriff's department. He put up a Skye Shay to steal your father's money."

"She claims she found your father's body, but left without looking for the money," Eleanor said.

"The money was already gone thanks to Faith," I said.

"So Faith was a thief?" Angelo asked.

"We'll have to assume so because we'll never know for certain. But the money was in the SUV."

"What still doesn't make sense to me, Agnes, is that if Faith was murdered at Wilber's house, who drove the SUV back to Neiman's?"

"It must have been Earle," I said. "Can you think of anyone else who would think to steal from your father, Angelo?"

"I suppose you think I did it. I had a problem with drugs some time ago."

My eyes widened. "Honestly, I don't think you did it. If you wanted to steal from your father you could have done it at any time."

"He kept it close to him," Angelo said. "I don't think he ever fully trusted me after my drug issue."

"We saw you two go to your father's house after his body was found. Were you looking for the money?"

Callie gasped and exchanged a look with her brother. "Angelo was worried about the money."

"I was worried it would be stolen before we had possession of the property," Angelo insisted. "Especially with that neighbor of his across the street."

"Robert Boyd?"

"That's the one. He was always watching my father's place. That and a young woman who was over occasionally." Angelo looked disgusted. "I saw her hanging all over the Hill brothers recently. I wouldn't be surprised if they tried to rip off our father."

"You must mean Robert and Gia, not the Hill brothers," I said.

"Yeah, the Hills aren't as poor as they act. Millionaires, from what I heard."

Eleanor and I burst out laughing. "Millionaires?" I said. "Believe me, the Hills are just as they appear. Country folks from down south."

"Ones who will shoot you if you trespass," Eleanor added with a curt nod.

"We'd better get going. Thanks again, you two."

I jumped in the vehicle and Eleanor asked, "We going to the Hills?"

"Shouldn't that be heading for the hills?" I joked. "And I was hoping we could catch up with Robert."

"I'll call the sheriff."

Eleanor and I parked along the shoulder of the road at Robert's house. The last thing I wanted to do was get trapped in Robert's driveway. The cops would do that when they arrived.

Robert's black truck with the lifters was parked in the back. There was no movement in the house.

"What should we do?" Eleanor asked.

"Knock on the door? I don't think Robert will think it amiss because we've come here before."

Eleanor knocked on the door, it wasn't answered. I let my partner pound on the door louder, but I was off the porch and heading to the truck.

"Wait up, Agnes. Where are you going?"

"To see if Robert is in the backyard."

I walked to the driver's side of the truck and stepped back at finding shattered glass on the ground. I looked up with a gasp at the bullet hole in the driver's side window.

"I think you might want to call the sheriff again," I said. "I can't see inside the truck, but I have a feeling that Robert's dead."

"We going to stick around or head out to the Hills' place to find Gia?" Eleanor asked. "I have a feeling that she'll be packing her bags."

Eleanor didn't have to make the call. Sheriff Peterson's car led a posse of cop cars four strong roaring into the driveway.

Peterson lowered his window. "Did you find Robert?"

"Nope, but I don't think he's going anywhere."

"We believe he might be dead in his truck," Eleanor said.

"There's a bullet hole in the window. I can't see inside with those lifters."

"Stay here," Peterson warned.

This is one time I planned to obey his command.

Peterson and his deputies pulled their side arms and approached the truck. Peterson opened the door and Robert's body tumbled to the ground, quite dead.

Eleanor and I edged to our vehicle. The sheriff wouldn't be able to leave the scene now, and we had to catch up with Gia before she got away.

I drove off in a hurry just as two state police cruisers pulled up. They weren't concerned with us -- they had an active crime scene.

Eleanor and I walked up to the Hill house, and I peered in the back screen door. Gia was holding a gun on Rosa Lee, but I couldn't see either Curt or Curtis.

"Tell me where you're hiding your money, old lady."

"That's no way to talk to me after I rented a room to you -- and real cheap too."

I motioned to Eleanor with a finger covering my lips. I then pointed for her to go. Eleanor had the good sense to call the sheriff if I could get her to budge from the corner of the house.

I pulled back and quickly joined Eleanor around the corner of the house when I heard footsteps near the door.

Rosa Lee walked outside, followed by Gia, who held a gun to the back of her head. Rosa Lee carried an oversized suitcase to the back of the Hill brothers' truck and did her best to throw it in the bed. I swallowed the lump in my throat. If Rosa Lee was outside, where were Curt and Curtis?

I tried the front door, but it was locked. The Hills didn't use the front door as a matter of routine. I couldn't wait any longer. I had to help Rosa Lee and leave Eleanor to find the boys.

I whispered instructions to Eleanor. She shook her head, but I gave her a gentle shove to the back door.

"Hello, Rosa Lee," I said as I approached the truck.

Gia turned with a snarl and grabbed the back of Rosa Lee's shirt as she pointed the gun at me.

"You picked the wrong time to come calling."

"Oh, but I'm not here to visit. I'm here to bring you in for killing Wilber and Faith." I nodded to Rosa Lee as if I could calm her nerves.

"That's a laugh. You might want to talk to Robert about that. I can hardly put a body in a barrel and hide it on Wilber's property."

"I knew it," I cackled. "You admitted where Faith's body was concealed. If you were after Wilber's money why kill Faith?"

"Because my stupid sister took the money before I had the chance to steal it. I still can't believe she killed Wilber. Apparently I underestimated her."

"Oh come on. How stupid do you think I am? Faith didn't kill

Wilber. He saw the blood on the carpet and you worried that he'd call the police."

"I still don't understand why he didn't, but then again if he called the cops and they found my sister's body they'd think he killed her."

"So who drove the SUV back to Neiman's?"

"Robert did. I was too busy here trying to con these stupid hillbillies."

"Now that's not politically correct," I said with a shake of my head. "So what's this I heard about the Hills supposedly having money?"

"I know they're loaded."

"Locked and loaded perhaps."

"That's what I told her." Rosa Lee laughed. "Could you let go of my shirt, Gia? I already told you I don't have any money. I grow my own vegetable and make all my meals."

"She's right about that. Hey, where are Curt and Curtis?"

"I shot them. They'll hopefully bleed out before the cops show up."

"That will happen sooner than you think. They know where I am and will show up very soon now."

"Get in the truck before I shoot the both of you."

"Not worried about the money anymore? I can't say I blame you."

Rosa Lee climbed in the truck first. Gia sat between us and ordered me to drive.

"I can't drive this truck. It's too big!" I gasped.

"Get moving before I lose my temper and shoot your friend."

"That's not very neighborly," I said as I turned the key and the engine roared to life. The truck was hardly quiet. I always knew when they were barreling down the road before seeing the Hill brothers.

I backed up into Rosa Lee's swing. "Sorry," I apologized.

"Not a problem. I'll have my boys fix it for me."

I drove to the end of the driveway praying that the cops were there, but I was mistaken. I raced up the road. I knew all the back roads. But did I really want to drive on them when it would only make it easier for Gia to dump our bodies? I turned down a dirt road and bit my bottom lip as I drove over the ruts. The truck had too much power for me and it fishtailed.

"So Faith is your sister and you didn't even involve her in your scheme," I said.

"Blood isn't thicker than money."

"You gotta love a sick and twisted family. Is Robert related to you too?"

"We're married -- or were."

"Why did you kill Robert when he helped you?"

"I'm covering my tracks. Nobody would have ever suspected me of anything when I've been hanging all over the Hill brothers."

"Oh, so you're the brains of the operation."

"I still can't believe I worried about her taking my boys away from me," Rosa Lee said.

"I did. I killed them."

"We'll see."

"Getting back to your plot, Robert should have checked the SUV before he brought it back. Faith hid the money in the vehicle. Eleanor and I found it."

"Turn there," Gia said as she glared at me.

"There isn't anything back there but swamp," I protested.

"Good place to hide bodies."

"It's not like you'll be able to get away with this," I said. "You told us you killed Curt and Curtis."

"My boys ain't dead," Rosa Lee said.

"Believe me, they're both dead," Gia shouted as she ordered us out of the truck.

"Get walking."

I swallowed hard as we were headed straight for a swampy area. The sound of frogs and buzzing mosquitos filled my ears. "This is as far as I can walk," I said.

Gia poked my back with the gun. "Keep moving."

I turned and faced her. "I'm not moving anywhere," I insisted.

Gia raised her gun and Rosa Lee smiled. Was she happy I was about to get my brains blasted out?

Click ... click .... click.

"Sounds like you're all out of bullets," I said.

Rosa Lee pulled bullets from her pocket and threw them into the swampy water.

Gia growled and moved to shove Rosa Lee to the ground, but I got between them and received the blow. I groaned when I hit the ground. I focused on Gia and looked helplessly at her foot as she moved to kick me in the stomach. I closed my eyes tightly and heard a voice. "Better back off now, I don't want to have to shoot you," Curt said as he pointed his shotgun at Gia.

"Not such stupid hillbillies after all," I said with a smirk as Curtis helped me up.

Curt didn't waver despite the bullet wound to his shoulder.

"Where did you boys come from?" I asked.

"Hiding under the tarp," Curt said.

"We were waiting for the right moment to pounce," Curtis said. "If you wasn't a girl I'd knock you to the ground, Gia. Nobody treats Ma like that."

"And to think she rented you a room," Curt said. "She won't be doing that no more."

"Now that, boys, is something I can agree with." Rosa Lee laughed.

I was concerned about the gunshot wounds both Curt and Curtis suffered. Curt had a wound to his shoulder and a bullet grazed Curtis' head. Gia had nearly killed the brothers.

A siren cut on, and I was thankful when Sheriff Peterson climbed out of his cruiser. I elbowed Gia, and she slammed into the side of the cop car. "Oops," I said. "Paybacks."

EPILOGUE

Eleanor and I were sitting in Curt and Curtis's hospital room as several pretty nurses fussed over them. They grinned, loving the attention, even though a few hours ago they professed to have given up on women.

"So what's this about you Hills being millionaires?" I asked.

Rosa Lee shook her head. "Of all the far-fetched stories."

"I thought that too when I heard it. I forgot to ask Sheriff Peterson how he found us so quickly."

"We have a tracking device on our truck," Curt said. "If you'll remember, we help the FBI out on occasion."

"I'll have to thank my son Stuart for involving you, but it's not as if you weren't hiding in the back of your truck. How did you manage to do that without Gia seeing you?"

"We snuck out of the house and hid when Gia was with Ma in the kitchen. It was the longest twenty minutes of our lives," Curt said.

"I don't want to think about what would happen if anyone hurt our Ma," Curtis said.

Andrew and Mr. Wilson walked in the door.

"They didn't have anything good in that cafeteria," Mr. Wilson grumbled as he pushed his rolling walker along.

Andrew set down a tray and handed out coffees. "We'll stop by Tim Hortons tomorrow before we come up," he promised.

"Aw, I hope we won't still be in the hospital tomorrow," Curt complained. "Not that I don't like the company."

We laughed. "Settle down, boys. I think you forget the nurses are only doing their job," Rosa Lee said.

There was a knock on the door and Bernice walked in. Her face had a little more color than the last time I saw her.

"I'm so sorry you boys were hurt," Bernice cried.

"Don't you dare blame yourself, Bernice," Rosa Lee admonished her. "I'm the ninny that rented a room to … that Gia."

"I still can't believe this was all because Wilber kept a little cash at home," Bernice said.

"What do you consider a little cash?" Eleanor asked.

Bernice shrugged. "Give or take twenty thousand, or so Wilber told me."

I gasped. "There wasn't that much money in the bag we found."

"Probably not. Wilber hid most of it where nobody will ever find it."

"Which is where?"

"With me. He gave it to me to hold on to. I should have known something was going on when he started getting paranoid. He believed someone was stealing from him. I didn't think much of it because Wilber had been known to get like that sometimes."

"Except he wasn't wrong this time," I said. "Did you give the money to Angelo and Callie yet?"

"What, and stop them from digging up the crawl space to find it? Not on your life." She cackled. "Teach them to treat me like they have. I'll give them the money eventually."

"So how is it going with your children now?"

"They're trying, and so am I, but I don't harbor any false expectations."

"It takes time. How are you feeling?"

"Much better. And I'm back at home. Elsie didn't much care that my cats camped out over her place."

I smiled because the visual was too good.

I was sad that Wilber was gone and that Bernice would never know what might have been. It made me all the more thankful that I had my Andrew, who I hugged extra close after my ordeal.

"One thing I'm thankful for is that Wilber wasn't a serial killer," Bernice said. "It was hard thinking about him that way."

"I believe the residents of Tawas think that way too. We don't want to be remembered as the town where a serial killer once lived."

I sipped my coffee and watched Rosa Lee's warm face as she sat between her sons' beds. She hadn't left the hospital since they'd arrived and there was no amount of talking that would ever change that. I still had to smile when I thought about anyone considering them millionaires, but then there was always that moment when I thought ... well, what if?

ABOUT THE AUTHOR

USA Today Bestseller Madison Johns is most known for her Agnes Barton Senior sleuths mystery series featuring lively and zany senior citizen sleuths — Agnes Barton and Eleanor Mason. Her time working at a nursing home was all the inspiration she needed to portray realistic characters that readers have gone on to love. Her first book Armed and Outrageous has solidified her in the publishing world and her series has been well received.

Madison's aim was simple; she wanted to change how the world viewed senior citizens. Why you could take a stroll through her neighborhood in Mid-Michigan where some of the liveliest seniors live to know she wasn't that far off the mark.

She knew if she used what she had learned while caring for senior citizens to good use, it would result in something quite unique.

She now works full time as a writer from home where she continues to write cozy mysteries.

Visit her on the web at: http:/www.madisonJohns.com. Sign up for Madison's mystery newsletter list to receive new release alerts at http://eepurl.com/4kFsH.

OTHER BOOKS BY THIS AUTHOR

Armed and Outrageous
Grannies, Guns & Ghosts
Senior Snoops
Trouble in Tawas
Treasure in Tawas
Bigfoot in Tawas
High Seas Honeymoon
Outrageous Vegas Vacation
Birds of a Feather
Undercover Inmates
Camping Caper
Hawaiian Hangover
Scandal in Tawas
Tawas Goes Hollywood

An Agnes Barton Paranormal Mystery Series
Haunted Hijinks
Ghostly Hijinks
Spooky Hijinks
Hair-Raising Hijinks

OTHER BOOKS BY THIS AUTHOR

Ghastly Hijinks

An Agnes Barton Holiday Mystery
The Great Turkey Caper
The Great Christmas Caper
Lucky Strike

Kimberly Steele Sweet Romance
Pretty and Pregnant
Pretty and Pregnant Again

An Agnes Barton/Kimberly Steele Romance
Pretty, Hip & Dead
Petty, Hip & Hoodwinked
Pretty, Hip and Venomous

A Cajun Cooking Mystery
Target of Death

Lake Forest Witches
Meows, Magic & Murder
Meows, Magic & Manslaughter
Meows, Magic & Missing
Meows, Magic, & Mayhem
Meows, Magic & Wands
Meows, Magic & Elves

Kelly Gray Sweet Romance
Redneck Romance

Paranormal Romance

Clan of the Werebear
Clan of the Werebear, the Complete Series

Shadow Creek Shifters

OTHER BOOKS BY THIS AUTHOR

Katlyn: Shadow Creek Shifters
Taken: Shadow Creek Shifters
Tessa, Shadow Creek Shifters
Llama and the Lady

Western Historical Romance

Nevada Brides Series
McKenna
Cadence
Kayla
Abigail
Penelope

Brides for the Bart Gang
Nevada Sunrise
Nevada Sunshine

Johanna, Bride of Michigan, is 26th in the unprecedented 50-book, American Mail-Order Brides series
Johanna: Bride of Michigan

Printed in Poland
by Amazon Fulfillment
Poland Sp. z o.o., Wrocław